LIMESTONE WALL

LIMESTONE WALL

Marlene Lee

For Bill, a friend indeed, and to Alice, thank you for your loyalty! As ever, Marlene

Holland House

www.hhousebooks.com

Copyright © 2014 by Marlene Lee

Marlene Lee asserts her moral right to be identified as the author of this book. All rights reserved. This book or any portion thereof may not be reproduced or used in any manner whatsoever without the express written permission of the publisher except for the use of brief quotations in a book review.

All characters appearing in this work are fictitious. Any resemblance to real persons, living or dead, is purely coincidental. Any characters denoted by government office are entirely fictional and not based on any official, appointed or elected.

Excerpt from 'A Lesson Before Dying' Copyright (c) 1993 by Ernest J. Gaines. Permission by G Agency LLC.

Hardback ISBN: 978-1-909374-33-1
Paperback ISBN: 978-1-909374-34-8
Epub ISBN: 978-1-909374-35-5

Cover design by Ken Dawson
http://www.ccovers.co.uk/

Typeset by handebooks.co.uk

Published in the USA and UK

Holland House Books
Holland House
47 Greenham Road
Newbury, Berkshire RG14 7HY
United Kingdom

www.hhousebooks.com

For Barbara, Judy, Priscilla, and Sandy

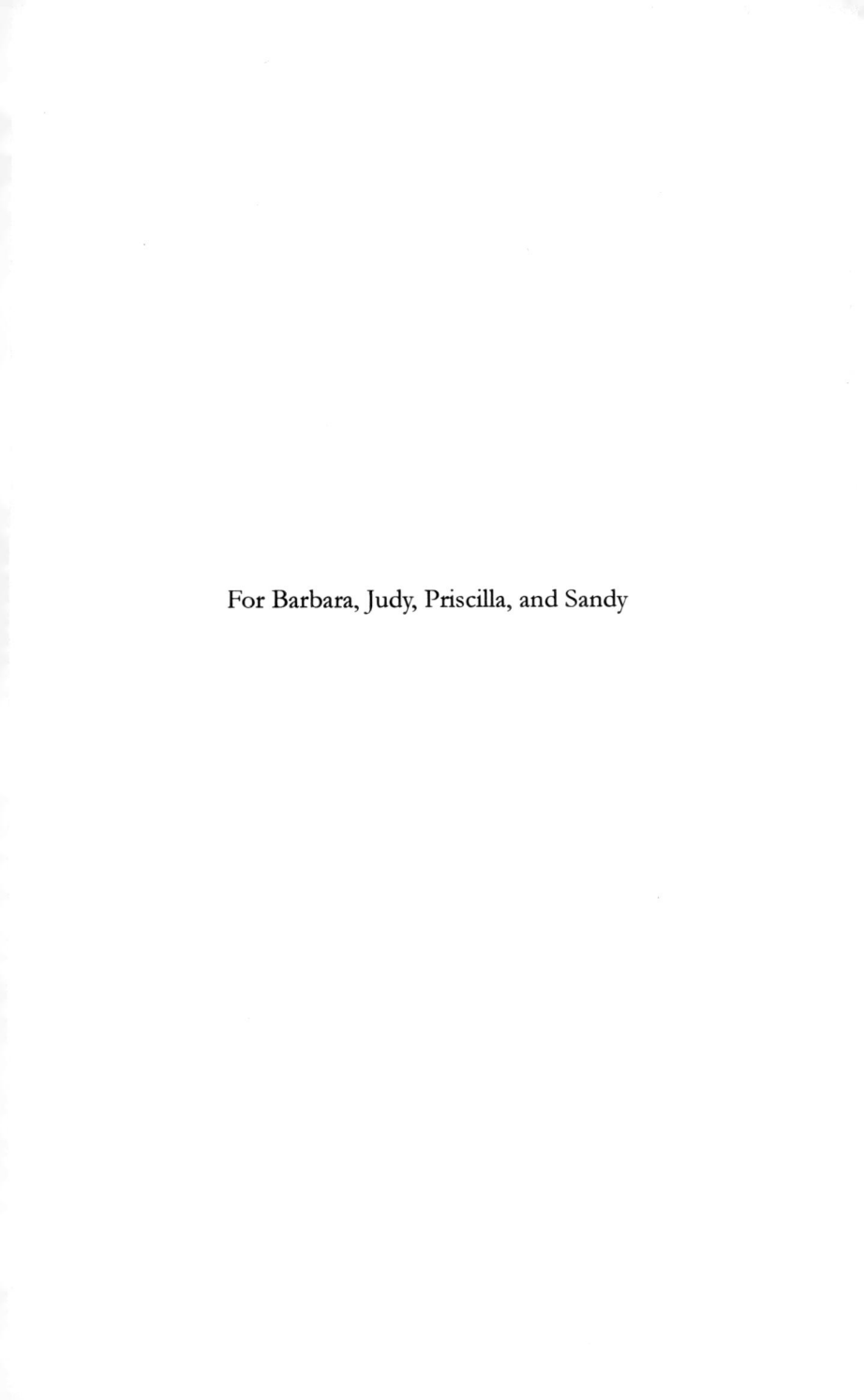

Prologue

By 2010 the original prison is gone. Only H-Hall still stands, the oldest building in the oldest prison west of the Mississippi. Portions of the limestone wall remain, broken up to show tourists the rebar and construction rubble still packed inside. Executions have been moved to Southern Missouri. There are tours now, and the original gas chamber is popular. People like to go inside and pretend, for a few minutes, that they're condemned. From my front room I look out at the rusting guard towers and think back to when the limestone wall disappeared behind our closed drapes every evening and reappeared each morning, before my mother was taken away.

One

I couldn't see the Missouri Penitentiary from the train station, but I'd felt the beat of its limestone heart all the way from the Mississippi River to the center of the state. New York City seemed very far away.

In front of the depot I kept my head down and walked toward the waiting taxi. Leaving my bags at the curb—"Can you give me a minute?"—I stepped back inside the waiting room, empty except for the man behind the caged ticket window. In a water-stained corner of the ceiling, pounded tin hung loose. I missed the rumble of baggage carts and telegraph clatter that used to fill the place. But the marble floor seemed friendly, as smooth as when I'd played jacks, onesies through tensies, waiting with my mother for the Missouri Pacific.

"I'm going to the Missouri Hotel," I said, outside again.

"I wouldn't do that," said the driver.

"Why not?"

"It burned down years ago."

Steve Mason hadn't mentioned the fire.

"There are motels on the highway," he added.

"That far out?"

"The highway runs through town now." Amused, he opened the back door for me. "When was the last time you was in Jefferson City?"

"1959."

"Forty-some years ago?" He gave a long, low whistle and got in behind the wheel. The taxi smelled sour. Cold cigarettes and sweat. "Where you headed?"

"Capitol Avenue."

He started the engine. Blackheads studded the back of his neck but the cotton shirt collar was clean and pressed. "Where on Capitol?"

"Across from the penitentiary." He hitched himself around to face me, a sedentary man with a bad back. "The old one? Prison's moving east of town."

"The one that's always been on Capitol."

He faced forward again. "It's still there. They haven't moved the old guys out yet. Old guys and one old woman." He eased away from the curb and we turned south, uphill. Monroe Street passed by at a slant. "Lots of activity right now. I can't get you to the gate."

Ahead, the First Methodist Church opened its arms. "What kind of activity?"

"Execution next week. Protestors."

"Can you swing through town?"

At seven-thirty it was still light. The three dime stores, Woolworth, Kress, and Newberry, were gone. Still, turn-of-the-century buildings continued to gaze down on High Street, their brick facades ruddy with sunset. When five people wearing summer fabrics emerged from a restaurant and stepped onto the empty sidewalk, I shielded my face and moved to the middle of the seat.

"For now, they're gonna keep the old prison open for tourists. That, and the gas chamber. The execution's this Wednesday. Darn right."

"712 Capitol Avenue," I said. I wanted to be near the prison walls, the Capitol dome, the Methodist Church steeple, the county courthouse. Give me the old part of town: High Street. Monroe. The Lafayettes and Madisons, Marshalls and Jacksons. No subdivisions. No malls.

June air carried hymn-singing from the direction of the prison. A fifty-ish woman walked her dog west on Capitol, and I studied her as if we were survivors from the same refugee camp, as if there were rumors: *The person you're looking for walks a dog every evening*, or *You'll find the person you long for in a taxicab approaching the Missouri State Penitentiary.*

"Why did they leave one old woman behind?"

"Don't know. It was in the paper, though." The sound of singing and chanting grew louder. The taxi slowed. "I can't get any closer." Ahead, a crowd blocked the way.

"Can you let me off at the corner? I'll only be a minute." Stepping onto the pavement, I brushed against one of the orange-and-white-striped sawhorses stenciled "Missouri State Prison." In front of the entrance a line of police stood at attention, the only bodies that weren't moving and swaying in the hymn-thick air. At the edge of the crowd I passed a solitary gentleman in khaki walking shorts who stood slightly apart, thin legs knotted with varicose veins. In slow motion he raised a sign, neatly printed: " 'God bless us every one.' Tiny Tim."

Across from my old house, the prison wall sat cooling in encroaching twilight. Behind the administration building, prison dormitories were hidden from view, sunk below grade in the old quarry that had furnished rock for the entire enterprise. All my life the state penitentiary had been just across the street. I remembered touching the warm, rough limestone when I was a child, curling my hand around the strand of salad called ivy as it crawled up the wall. My mother rushed across the street, grabbed me by the arm, and dragged me back to our front lawn. Never go near the prison! Pray for the prisoners, but only from our side of the street!

A siren in one of the guard towers began a paralyzing slide up the scale. Startled, I leaped in place, blocked by a line of protestors holding a banner at waist height—"Born-Agains for Tim"—and vigorously singing "Jesus Loves Even Me." A middle-aged woman with a severe haircut held a megaphone in one hand and beat time with the other. Beside her, a young man stepped toward me. "Join us?" he asked.

I shook my head.

"It's Jefferson City at Armageddon," he explained. "This is the first execution we've had in years."

"I remember an execution when I was a child," I said. "This

5

is just one of many down through Missouri history." I sounded like someone commemorating capital deaths. Ahead, from the Cherry Street end of the block, more chanting wound between and around blasts from the megaphone. Above the wall, floodlights in the guard towers came on, obliterating early stars.

I was standing in front of my old home; lawyers' offices. Gone were the spirea bushes at the edge of the lawn. Ditto the hydrangeas. But the hickory tree, taller now, still grew at the property line. During summer vacations, Barbie and Jackie Pletz from next door came for picnics under its branches. Mrs Pletz's cheese sandwiches had been very different from my mother's egg salad. The mustard was strong enough to open up a space behind the nose as dark as a cave. Those sandwiches, foreign artifacts, were cut into four triangles instead of halves. The Pletz house had felt foreign, too: Purple carpeting with blue flowers; a fruity smell in the rooms, like old oranges; toys scattered about. The house had seemed careless and tolerant of mistakes.

At about that time, my flat world began to grow round. At age seven or eight, I realized my neighbors and my neighbors' neighbors were different from one another. Households were not alike. My family was distinct from every other family. My mother was not like other mothers.

"How's the prison look?" the driver asked as I reached the corner and climbed into the back seat again. "About the same?"

I nodded.

He stuck his head out the window and made a U-turn. "I don't suppose you've got anyone behind the walls."

The black vinyl felt sticky. I kept my hands in my lap.

"What you was asking about, the Missouri Hotel," he went on, "it was arson. A couple of prisoners escaped and set the place on fire. Of course, it was already boarded up. No one stayed there anymore, not even on State business."

Early one evening, perhaps the very day of the cheese and egg salad sandwiches, as I walked to the playground through sleepy coos of mourning doves, the penitentiary had come to life behind me. Had I heard someone talking about a prison break or an execution? A riot? Had I caught a glimpse of my future? Whatever the reason, the giant across the street stirred and began to breathe. Its breath fluttered the curtains at every window in my neighborhood. That day I realized the prison had always been inhaling and exhaling; I'd just never heard it. I forced myself to keep going, but as soon as I reached the playground, I turned and ran back home where my parents sat in front of the new TV set, watching yellowish-green images behind the plastic film they'd installed to protect the family's vision.

"Come here, Evelyn," my mother said. "The Methodist minister is on television."

"Sit down," my father said. "Your mother wants you to watch the service." I sat on the floor between them, not too close to the screen because my mother said even with the green plastic film, you never knew what damage a TV could do. But by the time the organ had stopped playing so the minister could talk, my father and I were drifting upstairs, he to his study and medical journals, a doctor who hadn't been able to cure his wife, and I to my dollhouse. Once she got caught up in prayer, my mother didn't notice whether anyone else was there or not.

"Forty years," the taxi driver said. "What brings you back now?"

"This and that," I said. "Tying up loose ends." *I'm a widow now*, I might have added, or *I want to know why my mother did what she did*, or simply: *I still love her.*

On my first morning back in Jefferson City I sat on the edge of the motel bed, its sweaty, unfresh sheets knotted under me. A headache hung on. I felt feverish.

"Information," I said into the telephone, wanting much more than the recorded message I received: prison visiting hours, 1:00 to 4:00. On an answerphone I left my name, the prisoner's name, and our relationship.

After coffee in the motel lobby, I called a cab. By noon I was standing in front of 712 Capitol. Energetic new demonstrators had replaced yesterday's late crew. The police were changing shifts, too, and I watched fresh reinforcements file to the wall from patrol cars blocking off Cherry. Below the nearest manned tower, a line, mostly women, waited at the prison entrance notched into the wall. They looked experienced, knowledgeable about penitentiaries and themselves. Envying them because they knew how to visit a prisoner, I got in line.

I looked west down Capitol Avenue where a new apartment building cast its out-of-scale presence over the neighborhood. In his letter, Steve had told me to expect the height, the glass and steel. He'd built it on the lot where his family's home once stood. Still, I was surprised by its power and modernity. I spotted a pay phone near the double doors to the prison and considered calling him, but he would hear the singing and megaphone and guess where I was. Standing in line, even with my headache and fever, provided comfort: these women would not know me or judge me.

My old bedroom window across the street was blank. No curtain, no shade, just glass with a glint of sunlight. Downstairs, the lawyers had decorated. Painted shutters were pulled aside to frame flowers and figurines. Forty years ago my mother moved behind that glass, occasionally coming forward to adjust a drape or dust a sill. I longed for her to come to the window.

At one o'clock the prison doors opened and they let us in. After giving up my driver's license and being stamped on the back of the hand with purple ink, I took a seat in one of the orange plastic chairs that filled the waiting room. Two officers kept watch over us; there were approximately thirty of us there to visit. I'd traveled two days by train for this moment, but now I wanted to be somewhere else. My headache and flushed face occupied me. I hoped I was just overwrought, not sick and infecting the women who sat feeding their children, wrapping and rewrapping crying infants in blankets soiled from Department of Corrections buses the State ran on schedules from Kansas City, St. Louis, and Springfield.

I changed position on the molded chair. Next to me, a baby girl nursed. Her miniature gold-and-pink-gemmed earrings glittered with each pull at the breast. On her infant forehead, a sweat of salty dew had broken out. Exhausted by the hard work of feeding, her ecstatic eyes rolled up into her head.

I labored under the weight of dead air in the room. Drawing a deep breath required effort. My attention roamed among the women's sandals and toenails, the room's dirty windows, the pulse in my temple.

Was my mother being ushered toward me at this very moment? Did she dread seeing me? Would she even come? I tried to remember what she looked like and failed. I shouldn't have come back to Jefferson City. The few letters I'd written had never been answered. Maybe they'd never been delivered. Was I going to mention them to her? Should I? Does one talk about the mail to one's mother? Would she know me? Should I introduce myself? Would it be rude to ask her why she destroyed our family?

The other women in the waiting room were much younger than I. My mother had been locked away for more years than these girls on orange plastic furniture had lived. I tried to grasp the fact that the brownish-green floor and ceiling, the dirty walls, had been here all along. These same Missouri windows were admitting smudged light the day my mother's cell door swung shut behind her.

On Sunday afternoons we would walk along pleasant, dappled streets named Fairmount, Moreau, Elmerine, Moreland. Leafy trees touched each other high above slow, occasional cars. Off Fairmount Boulevard, McClung Park overlooked the valley between the east side of town and High Street. We stood motionless, gazing across the distance at the domed Capitol. The county courthouse, quaint and beautiful, lifted its clock tower high above our town. If the wind was right, we heard its bell ring the hour. As my mother took my hand and we turned back for the long walk home, I thought life would be an endless succession of Sunday afternoons.

My face felt hotter now. Chill sweat dampened my arm pits and bra line. These women on plastic chairs knew who they were visiting. They had not waited forty years to talk to a stranger.

A voice announced the bus that would carry them to the new prison where their young men had already been moved. Eventually the old prison would be cleared out.

Someone called my name. My heart beat faster, and I couldn't stand. The guard repeated himself. I tried to control my breathing; I didn't want to be panting when I came face to face with her.

I followed the officer down a liver-colored hallway and entered a room where glass panels separated inmates from civilians. He pointed me to a booth and tall, three-legged stool. I climbed onto it and waited. Next to me, the Hispanic woman, who hadn't gotten on the bus with the others, continued to nurse her child. I guessed at how her husband, deprived of those breasts, might feel while he watched.

I tried not to slip off the stool that rocked now and then on its uneven legs. If I tipped into the glass, I might accidentally touch my mother through the splintered window, cut both of us, land on her, even break one of her bones. After being in prison for forty years, she might be fragile. Some people are fragile at seventy; some aren't.

Behind the glass, a guard with a crew-cut and florid face opened the door, stepped through, and picked up the telephone hanging on the wall. "Mrs Grant will not be coming for visitation today."

I listened through the receiver at my end and stared blankly.

"Mrs Grant will not be coming today," he repeated. He

looked down at a carbon copy and read, "Reason for refusal: inmate preference."

My stool wobbled. I put one foot on the floor and shook with the effort to neither sit nor stand. "Why?"

"I have no other information." The officer watched me closely, as if I, like my mother, belonged in a cell. I would have been happy to turn myself in. There was no particular reason to remain on the street side of the limestone wall. I hung up the telephone and climbed onto the stool again.

"You'll have to leave now," he said, bending slightly for better eye contact.

I all but crawled back to the waiting room. Someone was moaning: me. An alarm rang. A female guard took me through an unmarked door to a private room, and after sorting through a basket of driver's licenses, she found mine, gave me a Kleenex, and escorted me through the double doors onto the steps of the front entrance. I wanted to run, leave this place far behind, but I turned an ankle at the curb and had to limp across Capitol Avenue.

Two

I walked aimlessly up to High and back without any attempt to call a cab. Finally, after several round trips, my ankle felt better and my feet knew what to do. Of their own accord they took me toward 712 Capitol Avenue—past Mrs Winthrop.

Even in the 1950s she'd seemed like an old woman. One time she telephoned my mother and complained that I was taking short-cuts across her lawn and would I stop because I was wearing out the grass.

"She's screaming at me!" I'd sobbed one morning, aborting my walk to first grade and running back to the house. "Mrs Winthrop is screaming at me! I walked across her grass!"

My mother dropped the dust rag, pulled me up into the wing-back chair, and rocked me in her lap. "Now, now. She's a lonely, cranky old woman. We'll pray for her. Then we'll pray for her lawn." She laughed. "Last of all, we'll pray for your feet." She grasped my shiny sandal and wiggled it tenderly. "Dear God, please keep Evelyn's little feet off Mrs Winthrop's lawn."

I'd snuggled deeply into my mother's thighs, absorbing her yeasty smell and tenderness.

"We heard you were in town," Mrs Winthrop called from her porch, as if she'd been waiting half a century for me to pass by. "Are you back for good?"

"Just for a visit."

She moved down her property, apparently hearing and seeing perfectly. Her face had loosened and lost the high flush I remembered. She glanced toward the penitentiary. "Have you seen her?"

"Not yet."

"They're moving the pen farther east. They've kept her with

the men all these years."

"Why?"

Mrs Winston shrugged. "Even when the other women went to Tipton, she stayed. Maybe because she could run the X-ray. They trained her in the sick bay, you know." A mild breeze lifted dry, gray hairs off her head. "People said your father arranged it."

"My father died."

"This was before he left the country." Jefferson City might be the capital of the state, but outside the legislative halls, it was just another town on the river where people talked about each other.

I doubted my mother was ever trained on the X-ray. Who would trust her?

Mrs Winston's hands fluttered above the pouches of her breasts. "She's never left Jefferson City, you know."

In the 1950s my father was a medical consultant to the Department of Corrections. Perhaps he talked to someone in the prison system. If she'd gotten better—almost well?—he might have arranged for her to work in the hospital ward. Could Mrs Winthrop be right about the X-ray? Could he have trained my mother on the X-ray, himself? I imagined them laboring over equipment guidelines, manufacturer's instructions. How wonderful to think that my father never went to Mexico. Never abandoned his medical practice. Had not been lonely or ashamed. That he'd stayed on, a doctor behind walls, communicating easily with the Governor and the State, all the time watching over my mother. Never died. I almost believed it. Tears of gratitude seeped into my hot eyes. "Have you seen her?" I asked.

"She won't see anyone."

Mechanically I began walking again.

"She won't let anyone visit," Mrs Winston called after me. "Not even you."

I continued down the block until I stood in front of my

13

old house. Except for an outside staircase bristling off the east wall and a doorway upstairs, a cut and a slash into my parents' bedroom, it looked the same: two stories, red brick, with a mansard roof and crisp white window surrounds. The sign anchored in the front lawn read, "Glenn, Greenberry & Nixon, Attorneys at Law." I longed to go inside and find familiar furniture.

"May I sit in the waiting area for a few minutes?" I asked the young woman at the reception desk. "It used to be my living room."

She stared for a moment. My eyes must have been red. "You lived here?"

I nodded.

"When?"

"1950 to 1959."

She covered my hand with hers. "Would you like to see the house?"

I'd thought so, but the desk mindlessly blocking the fine curved staircase offended me. Perhaps if I sat quietly in the living room behind the deep-set windows, I could forget the offense; could forget the taxi ride this morning along the highway that split my town into unfamiliar halves like an injured brain whose two lobes have trouble making connections; could forget that my mother had just refused to see me.

The receptionist reached for the telephone. "Can you come out here, Mr Glenn?" She turned back to me. "Do you have children in Jefferson City? Grandchildren?"

"My kids live in California." I could have told her my husband died last year. That I had an old schoolmate in town named Steve Mason with whom I'd exchanged Christmas cards over the years. That he was on the committee for the centennial celebration of our grade school. That I no longer had the wherewithal to celebrate childhood. That coming back was a mistake.

The lawyer who came from the back of the house was the protestor from the born-agains I'd seen the evening before. His symmetrical features and close-shaved skin gave him a stable, community-minded look, as if he might coach six-year-olds on Saturday and the next day teach their Sunday School class. His single flaw—ears standing out from his head—confirmed his sincerity.

I extended a damp hand. "I'm Evelyn Grant Williams."

"Charles Glenn." He seemed too youthful to be one of the partners listed on the sign out front. His sympathetic "Welcome" annoyed me. After all, I'd lived here before he was born. "Are you—" he skimmed the room and ceiling with his eyes—"a Grant?"

I nodded.

His shoulders lost definition, then straightened. "We consider ourselves stewards of—the Grant home." He hesitated each time he was about to say 'Grant'. "You'll see a few changes."

"You seem too young to know much about the Grant home," I said.

"My partners know." He gestured toward the living room. "Let me show you around. We've made some changes, of course." On the way past the fireplace I heard a dog bark.

Pepper?

In place of the piano and piano bench where my mother had sat beside me keeping time, two upholstered armchairs monopolized the wall. The arched doorway leading out of the front room was still intricately carved in arabesques and pineapples, but what happened to the hutch in the dining room where we'd spread sheets of newspaper and polished the silverware? Instead of the industrial odor of silver polish, such a strong smell for such a little bit of gray paste in a tiny jar, I smelled the leatherbound books that lined the room: *Missouri Revised Statutes. Legislative Amendments to Supreme Court Rules.* I bent down to look under the conference table. He stooped, too. "Is there something under there?"

I straightened, slightly breathless from the exertion. "We had a dining room table with cabriole legs," I said. "Do you know what happened to it?"

"I don't."

"Do you think maybe it's stored upstairs?"

"That, I couldn't say." He put his hands in his pockets but immediately withdrew the left one to check his watch. "We completely renovated the kitchen," he said. "Come see."

"I don't want to take too much of your time," I said. "My parents bought the new dining room table just before Thanksgiving, probably 1956. We bought it at Milo Waltz Furniture. Are they still in business?"

When the Milo Waltz deliverymen had collected the soft pads protecting the high gloss of a new table, I'd squeezed my father's hand. "I can see myself in the furniture polish."

He and my mother ruffled my hair, touching me without touching each other. "Now you won't need a mirror," my father said. He left for his hospital rounds, my mother went up to the little sewing room in the walk-in closet, and I sat down under the new table to play house. I was the only one downstairs, but I knew how to play alone. Everyone in our family knew how to be alone. We knew how to concentrate, too. People who can be alone and concentrate are ahead of the game. My father said concentration was thinking; my mother said it was praying. Under the new dining room table I concentrated on the curved mahogany legs and round, knobby feet; on the fresh, orangish-yellow wood on the underside; on the mechanism for sliding the tabletop apart.

Now as I followed Charles Glenn into the kitchen, I remembered the 1950s sink and stove, the neighbor lady sobbing at the yellow Formica table, her head near the salt and pepper shakers, her gray hairs stuck in the butter dish. "Why? Why?" she screamed. My father stood by the back door, gray in the face. Smaller.

Running up the stairs, I heard him follow me. Before his foot touched the top step, I'd thrown myself into the walk-in closet and landed on my mother's prayer cushions. When he'd looked in all the rooms and finally found me lying on my stomach, he saw that the closet was no longer a sewing room. It had taken him months to learn what I already knew: that my mother, pushing aside fabric, scissors, and thread, had grasped the Singer sewing machine by its arm, dropped it into its nesting position below the tabletop, and laid a velvet cloth across what became an altar.

At first my father stood still, as if he weren't surprised to find a church in the closet. Then he slowly buckled onto his knees beside me. I heard his huge, wet breaths. His shaving lotion smelled like medicine. He moved about the walk-in closet on all fours, like an animal that needs to drink but is too sick to find water. He crawled back beside me and curled up on the floor. Slowly he turned his head toward me. Tears hung from the end of his nose. To me, he looked messy. I waited for Mother to come in with a handkerchief. I think he was waiting, too. But we would wait for the rest of our lives and she would never come. When he lay very still, I was afraid he'd died. So when he got to his feet, lunged for the cross on top of the sewing table, and hurled it into the corner, I was glad because I saw that he was going to live.

"Prayer!" he shouted. "Prayer! Look what it's done for her!"

Three

By the next day the stone wall and prison and crowds had become, if not familiar, less foreign. My speeded-up mind was beginning to decelerate. My mother didn't want to see me? I would train myself not to care. Matter-of-factly I would line up at visiting hours with the other women, be routinely refused, nonchalantly re-cross the street.

For a while after my husband died, grief had opened and closed with accordion action. The real Walter would thin. Give way to a copy. Become a substitute. An idea. There was relief, but then I would feel his fingertips at my wrist again and in my hair. At those times I would have been willing to die, myself, if I could have touched him one more time, traced a line from his pelvis upward to his shoulders, downward to his thighs. After a week of crying, my mouth's hunger would fade. Then the next week would roll by and I would be saturated with grief again.

Eventually I would learn not to think about my mother.

Steve's apartment building seemed a little less innovative today, less steel-and-glass. The crowds, too, were less vivid. Less energetic. They weren't singing and they weren't chanting. They didn't even mill about as they'd done yesterday. The signs looked limp and were not held high; the old gentleman, Tiny Tim, was gone.

I turned left onto Monroe. Just as I reached the courthouse, the skies opened and a hot June rain caught Jefferson City and me off-guard. The raindrops were so large and slow I considered running between them. They bounced off the pavement and beat on my head and heels. Crossing the wet grass, hurrying down a covered stairway leading to the courthouse basement, I heard the electric crack of lightning and smelled sulfur. It wouldn't have surprised me to see the clock tower, gargoyles, and snapped-off pieces of the courthouse lying about the lawn.

I stood at the basement door under a protective eave, rainwater running off my hair and clothes into the drain beneath. Water-logged twigs and debris lay against the basement door near patches of something fungus-like crawling into the corners of the below-grade entrance. I pictured, in quick succession, a furnace room behind me, a walled-up boiler, a storage closet with one dim light bulb swaying from a string, a jail cell. Just when I was getting warmed up—an ancient bathroom with a fetid toilet, a secret torture chamber—a police car pulled up at the curb. Ducking his head against the weather, an officer jumped out of the driver's seat, slammed the door, and ran up the courthouse steps. Rain turned to hail.

After a few minutes the hail stopped abruptly, as if the thought of ice had never crossed the mind of the sky. Normally, hailstorms would have left me wide-eyed and thrilled. See the danger we've come through! But I remained in the basement entrance, stunned. The officer, the police car, had released something, a whiff of damp dirt; body odor; even, strangely, shampoo. I stood paralyzed, dripping into the dirty rainwater that pooled around my sandals.

Forty years ago a police car pulled up in front of our house. Three officers jumped out and ran onto the porch through the rain. Someone had just washed their hair. My mother? Or maybe she'd washed mine. Maybe my hair was still wet, done up in kid curlers. But why would she wash and curl my hair if she was planning to run out the back door and do something that would ruin lives?

In my memory, the house grew still, secretive, a wary witness to something mysterious happening across the alley. The rooms developed lungs. They breathed.

My father may or may not have been at home when the patrol car arrived. My mother may or may not have already crossed the alley and re-entered our house. I may or may not have been standing at an upstairs window, my hair wet or not wet, in or out of curlers, when the police banged on the door.

If she'd wanted to kill someone, she could have killed me. She could have pushed me onto a bed and held a pillow over my face. She could have torn apart a kid curler and done something fatal with the wire inside. She could have killed her own child instead of someone else's babies. I'd already lived nine years; the twins had been alive for just a few months. In a way, I'd cheated them of their lives. I think I've always felt guilty: They were so little, so new; they were probably still learning to recognize their mother. They may have smiled up at this woman, feeling she loved them.

I ran downhill. I felt the courthouse moving away, rising higher and higher behind me. I thought I might have a heart attack. I turned the corner at the church and, ignoring the wet flapping of my skirt, stopped to catch my breath.

A man stepped from the steel-and-glass apartment building across Capitol. I stared at the lean face. Pausing on the sidewalk, car keys in one hand, he saw me. "Evelyn? Evelyn Grant?" By now I felt so unsteady that I sat down on the curb.

I was looking at a fifty-year-old man and at the same time seeing the grade-school boy. Steve Mason cocked his head to one side, a gesture I specifically associated with our fourth-grade cloakroom. I was surprised at how much he still looked like himself. He crossed the street. A weathered wrinkle in front of each ear tightened his skin and brought it cleanly up over the jaw. He seemed no more slack than he'd been in grade school, standing near the curb, looking down at me. "It's good to see you after all these years," he said, as if he weren't surprised to find me sitting at the edge of the street. "When did you get in?"

I pushed my wet hair off my forehead. There was nothing to be done about my sopping clothes and disreputable appearance. Was he remembering that I'd left school suddenly, my family in disarray? He offered his hand and I stood.

The teachers at Moreau Heights Elementary School had pitied me. "Evelyn is going to be leaving us today," Miss Schroer announced, laying the chalk in the chalk tray and walking up the aisle between desks in a grave procession of one. A tall woman in her fifties, she'd bent down to hug me. I've appreciated that gesture over and over through the years, though at the time, stunned and humiliated, it embarrassed me.

Steve shifted his weight. "Heck of a time for a school reunion." He waved his hand to take in the protestors. "Can I give you a ride?"

"I got caught in the rain," I said. I would ruin his car's upholstery. And where would I go? "I'm still dripping."

"Where are you staying?"

"In a motel on the highway."

"I'll drive you there."

I shook my head. I didn't want to leave Capitol Avenue.

"Let's see if Roz Teal is home." He smiled. "She'll fix you up."

I tried to make myself heard as we wove among demonstrators. "Thank you for your note about the centennial," I said. "Is Moreau Heights really a hundred years old?"

"Sure is. I did the research." I thought of the boy he had been, the shortest person in class, and the quickest. He was the one Miss Schroer would turn to in an emergency. If someone threw up, she'd say, "Quick, Steve. Run get Mr Brockman," and he would be off to get the janitor who stayed in the furnace room and came up only when someone vomited or when it was time to ring the brass hand bell at the end of recess. Now Steve was tall and slender, with a head of gray hair and the face of a man who likes to be outdoors. I learned that he'd worked in the Peace Corps. "In Pakistan," he said. "After that I worked out-of-state estimating cement volumes for some construction projects." He'd taken early retirement from the State of Missouri. He was divorced and had a grown son. "I'm a grandfather."

We stopped for a State trooper at Cherry and Capitol. Steve lifted his chin and studied me through his bifocals. "What about you? Except for a Christmas card now and then—"

"I moved to Idaho."

"Have you been back to see ..." He gestured toward the prison across the street. As soon as he'd spoken he looked uneasy. After all, he was an engineer, more comfortable with physical quantities than the fallout from a chance remark.

"My husband died last year," I said. It was no answer. He lowered his head with respect. "Actually," I said, "I've come back for more than the reunion. You're right. I'm here to visit at the prison."

He lifted his head. "You and Roz Teal have something in common." The trooper motioned us across the intersection. "She was in the class ahead of us. Did you know her?"

"I don't remember the name."

"She's been helping me with the centennial. A committee of two." We turned in to a house whose cracked driveway and sidewalk hosted flourishing clumps of grass. A woman was sitting on the porch.

"How are you, Roz? I've got a drowned specimen here who needs a towel."

The porch swing creaked as it gave up her weight. Roz Teal was heavy and awkward. In spite of a tank top, blouse, fringed shawl, it was obvious she had only one breast. Her hair was short and curly, between chestnut and red. She gave me a friendly scan, opened the screen door, and motioned me inside. While Steve remained on the porch, she and I went in search of a hair dryer.

"It's been a while since I've used it," she said, opening a cupboard here, a closet there. "I had cancer treatments," she continued cheerfully, "and didn't need a dryer. No hair."

"It's grown in nicely."

"Prettier than it used to be. Curlier, too. Let's see. Could it be—yes. Under the bathroom sink." She bent down and pulled out a dryer whose cord slithered across the tiles. She plugged it in, sat me down on the edge of the tub, and prepared to blast away.

"I can do that," I said.

"Nonsense. I used to be a hairdresser back in the dark ages. My brushes and combs are clean," she assured me, reaching for a plastic hairbrush. "I washed them just this morning. Must have known you were coming. Any particular style?"

I'm an average looking woman. I hadn't brought many clothes for my visit to Missouri. I didn't wear sunglasses or a veil at my husband's funeral. "I part my hair on the left," I said, and stopped talking. Earlier, on the porch, did she look into my red eyes and see I needed help?

Steve was sitting on the swing when we returned.

"Now if you'll throw me in the clothes dryer for half a cycle," I said, "I'll be presentable." He smiled. It wasn't the crooked and spontaneous smile of my husband, but still, it was nice. Subdued. Genuine. He stood so the two of us could sit on the swing.

"How are you holding up?" he asked Roz.

She drew a breath. Then, as easily, as immediately as a child, she wept. "I'm going to miss him so."

"Tim Anguin," Steve said in an aside. "All this excitement"—he gestured toward Capitol Avenue—"is about him."

"Oh, my," I said. So that was what we had in common. A murderer. Was Tim Anguin her son? Brother? Husband? She would know so much more than I about crime and the penitentiary. I backed away. "Thank you for the hair dryer," I said.

Steve stepped to the edge of the porch. "I'll look forward to seeing you soon. The reunion, if not before." I was preparing to leave, too.

"Oh," Roz said to me, sitting down again in the swing, "please stay a while." I didn't want to talk about Tim Anguin and the execution. I didn't want to stay, but she clearly longed for company. I watched Steve descend the porch steps.

I used to play house. Like most girls when they were little, I claimed a pretend husband and babies far in advance of when I would need them. While the clueless boys were racing their bicycles and oiling baseball mitts, I'd chosen Steve. I waved when he reached the mailbox.

When Roz saw that I wasn't going to join her on the swing—there wasn't much room—she sighed and got to her feet. "Coffee?"

"I came back to Jefferson City when I was married," she said once we'd reached the kitchen. "I'm fifty. Divorced."

Soon, I thought, she will tell me everything about herself.

Her house, she explained, was near Lincoln University. Though the college was now integrated, African-Americans still dominated the neighborhood. "My ex-husband is Simon Teal. You know, the black poet and professor Simon Teal. Have you read his work?"

"I'm sorry to say I haven't."

She set out coffee pot and cups before sitting down at the table. "Would you mind getting milk and sugar?" Apparently, once seated, she did not like to get up again. "Thank you, love. I prefer to sit. I don't exercise. I've just finished cancer treatment and I'm still tired." She handed me the cord to the coffeemaker. "Oddly enough," she said, pointing me to an electric outlet under the cabinet, "I have more energy when I'm away from home. Home makes me tired. That's why I'm almost never here. I'll probably never invite you back. Unless, of course, you need a hair dryer." More slowly she said, "When I found myself alone, ill, I began to do as I pleased. Even if people thought I was strange"—she gave me a piercing glance before looking idly about for, I guessed, a way to put water and coffee into the pot without getting up—"I began to do as I pleased."

I filled the pot at the sink and, without being told, rummaged in a cupboard for coffee.

"It's in the refrigerator," she said. "When I had cancer and when Tim lost his last appeal"—she prevented her face from crumpling, I saw the effort—"I gave up appearances. I don't care anymore what people think. Three heaping tablespoons. There are cookies in the cookie jar." The coffee began to perk. "So tell me: where do you live?"

"New York."

"And what brings you to Jefferson City?" The light shining through the kitchen window emphasized stress lines in her pale skin. Her face and head reminded me of a sculpture that's been through a flood.

"Nostalgia."

"What was your maiden name?"

"Grant."

By the time she'd told me about her master's in social work at Washington University and her marriage to Simon Teal, our coffee cups were nearly empty. Her parents, she said, stopped speaking to her when she married her husband, not because he was black, but because he wasn't Jewish. But where was she supposed to find a Jewish husband? If they'd wanted her to marry a Jew, they should have stayed in New York, on the Lower East Side. There weren't any Jews to speak of in Jefferson City. She met Simon and fell in love with him, but after they were married, he fell in love with another woman. She hated having her parents proved right about her marriage. Of course, they loved being right. Before they died she admitted to them they'd been right. Still, she said, maybe they hadn't been right. She wasn't sure, but the pleasures of the marriage had probably outweighed the pain of the divorce. Of course, it had taken years for her to reach this conclusion. Nevertheless—

"I had a good marriage and an ordinary adulthood," I said, touching on my job with the art gallery. I told her how, in my twenties, I'd stumbled onto a wise and stable man. "He died last year in a street accident."

Roz put her hands together, palm to palm, ten fingers pointing toward heaven, in a gesture of compassion. Then, "Would you top off our cups, Evelyn? Oh, and I heard Trixie scratching at the screen. Would you let her in?" As the cat strolled through the kitchen door, Roz said, "What was your maiden name again?"

"Grant." I hesitated. "I've come to visit someone in the prison."

She was keenly interested. "Who?"

The only woman in the penitentiary, I was about to say when her eyes widened.

"Mabel Grant. Of course." I waited for the eyes to narrow, turn blue-black with a sense of my strangeness. But when I looked into them, they were still sky-blue. "Your mother—it *is* your mother, isn't it?—has been here for years." How considerate of her to say "here," as if she were anywhere in Jefferson City but the state prison.

"I don't know her anymore," I said.

"You haven't visited her through the years?"

Silent, I stared at a stray coffee ground floating in my cup.

"Persevere," she said quietly. "I had to persevere with Tim." She sounded gratified by the experience, as if her effort weren't ending in the gas chamber on Wednesday. "Prison is its own world," she said. "I know. I've been teaching the literacy class for years." With palms on the table, elbows bent, she began executing her decision to stand. "We'll talk. I like to be part of everything that's going on. I know Jefferson City on both sides of the wall." She hauled herself to her feet. "You'll be comfortable here in no time."

I thanked her for the coffee, crossed through the dining and living room, and stepped onto the spongy boards of the porch. Trixie, who had escaped through the front door, followed as I picked my way down the paint-flecked steps that were pitched all wrong.

Four

On Saturday morning I returned to 712. The Glenn, Greenberry & Nixon office was open. I rang the bell at the unmanned reception desk.

"Do you have time to finish the tour?" I asked when Charles Glenn appeared from what used to be the downstairs bedrooms. "I know it's Saturday, but…"

His ears moved up, then down a fraction of an inch. "I have a little time," he said guardedly. I assured him I was ready to march briskly through the house. He looked pleased when I said, "We've done the kitchen. Let's move on." But behind the back stairs I lingered at the washer and dryer. "The laundry was always in the basement," I complained. I wanted to tell him about the manual washing machine downstairs, the way it squatted under a swaying light bulb, how it was surrounded by three tubs of rinse water with a wringer that, when released, swung from tub to tub. How you needed to be careful not to get your arm caught in it. I wanted to warn him that a high school girl in the neighborhood had a terrible scar, all puckered and buttermilk-colored, from catching her arm in the rollers. "The laundry was never on the main floor," I almost begged him. "It was always in the basement."

"Oh, we've renovated the basement. We framed in an apartment. It's all been rewired and replumbed."

I looked up toward the floorboards of my old bedroom. "Do you use the second floor?"

"No."

"Is it—empty?"

"No one lives there, if that's what you mean."

"Can I see it?"

"Mrs Grant—I mean Mrs Williams," and he made a gesture, a single swipe of the hand, as if cutting through the unthinkable, "we don't go up there."

"I've come all the way from New York," I said, a little desperate. I'd been deprived of my husband; my children were grown and in California; my mother was across the street in prison. It occurred to me that maybe some day I could bring her back across the street. Bring her home. I tamped down rising excitement. "Would you consider renting the second floor to me?"

"Rent? I don't know. It wouldn't be my decision." Leaning toward me, ears tilted forward, he seemed on guard against anything atypical. And maybe he was a little embarrassed by this strange request he would probably have to refuse. "I'd have to find the key," he said.

"Please."

Soon I found myself climbing the outside wooden staircase that hung like a growth on the east wall. Charles Glenn fumbled with the key ring and unlocked the door. Stepping through the new opening, a doorway that left the house cut and bleeding, I entered my parents' bedroom. The deep windowsills and twelve-foot ceiling hummed with their presence. My parents would never be incapacitated. They would never forget me. Our family would never change. I ignored Charles Glenn hurrying past.

When I caught up to him, he was opening and closing kitchen cabinets in what had been the sleeping porch. "I didn't know there was a kitchen up here," he said.

"There wasn't one," I said. "This was a sun porch. You've enclosed the porch."

"After all, it's been years—"

"Change is inevitable," I said without meaning it. The windows were probably stuck closed. Certainly there had been no air flowing through these rooms in years. I turned a faucet in the sink. The water sputtered, then ran brown before it cleared.

Did you really expect your house to be the same after all this time? I imagined my husband, Walter, saying. He'd been a quiet man, gentle and probing.

I didn't want to hold a conversation with him in front of the young lawyer. *Wait*, I said silently, and took the step down into the hall. But I was forced to stop at the landing. "When was *this* put in?" I wiggled a door knob.

"I'm not sure. Before my time." The young lawyer caught my distracted expression. "It's past history."

I looked out back where a golden retriever was dragging his leash through the sand and grit of the alley. The dog walked in the wheel ruts, criss-crossing the scraggily grass between. Underneath the room where I stood suspended over the back yard, my mother would be coming out of the house carrying a cardboard box. Soon she would step into view and walk toward the rusted barrel in the alley where, every week, she disposed of the paper trash. I already smelled the sharp, dirty smoke slinking up from the burn can.

Charles Glenn coughed a dry, short cough. "I'd better be getting back to work," he said, and took my arm. When we reached a doorway I stopped and looked at the closet door set into the far wall. The brass knob was tarnished. Mottled patterns in old varnish resembled a landscape; a faded fresco.

"May I stay up here a minute longer?"

"You're quite attached to the second story."

"Just for another quick look around."

Uncertainty disturbed his symmetrical face before he handed me the key. "You can bring it back when you're finished. I'll be here a while longer."

As soon as he left, I went to the door of the walk-in closet and put my hand on the brass knob.

Are you sure you want to do this? Walter murmured. I felt his hand, muscular and arousing, restrain mine. His words were patient. Skeptical.

You can see that I'm living in the present, Walter, I said. I recognize wheel ruts and garbage cans. I know a golden retriever when I see one.

Do you really expect your house to be the same after all this time, sweetheart?

I want it to be! I'm looking for my home, Walter!

But darling, your home is in New York.

Without you, Walter, it's not home!

You have the children... He began to withdraw, like our grown son and daughter when a phone call lasts too long.

Yes, yes, I said, and started to tell him that our daughter-in-law was pregnant and to beg him to stay with me a little longer.

Why are you standing here at the closet, Evelyn?

I'm looking for my mother.

Be here now, Evelyn. In life he'd never uttered clichés.

Without you, Walter, I don't know how. Please don't go.

The children, he said, slipping into an ethereal loop. *You have the children...*

I turned the knob, entered, and closed the door behind me.

The walk-in closet smelled of cedar, dust, and unpleasantness from a sour pile of stained throw rugs in one corner. I squinted. No sewing machine. No prayer cushions, altar, or cross. No reproduction of The Last Supper on the wall. Subsequent owners would have cleared everything out, and the house might have stood empty for years, maybe vandalized, sold at a loss. I know I'd never received any inheritance.

The wainscoting climbed half-way up the walls. When I was young it had stopped at eye level; now it ended at my elbow. Strips of molding still clung to the ceiling. The cedar floor needed sweeping. And, of course, the dirty rugs. My mother would never have permitted such a filthy stack. I imagined, rather than specifically remembered, sunlight through the window or, at night, the electric light in the ceiling, burned out now; I'd punched the black-and-white buttons on the old switch plate. I could imagine a policeman on May 22, 1959 lifting the sewing machine arm to look underneath for clues, but when I tried to remember him or tried to remember the machine's whir, its whine, see my mother's hand on the wheel, watch her thread the flash of silver, control the cloth ahead of the needle, I failed.

Sober now and alert, I feared what I might become: isolated, brooding, terrifyingly prayerful like my mother. I reached for the door knob. The door stuck from humidity and disuse. My blood pressure rose. It was a struggle to get out.

I hurried to the outside landing and down the stairs. Seated on the bottom step, I hung onto the banister post, perspiring and staring at patches of ivy climbing the prison wall. I should just go home to New York. Jefferson City was like a bad mother an abused child clings to. These rooms would punish me: remind me that my original family had disintegrated. But if I could come back to 712 Capitol Avenue, this time hold the center together... I stood up from the step, took out my checkbook, and went inside to pay young Mr Glenn and his partners whatever monthly rent they might ask.

On the first Sunday in town I crossed the street to the prison. "I'm here for Mrs Mabel Grant," I said, in no mood to dally; I had immediate plans. A three-month lease to the second floor of 712 was tucked in my purse. The corrections officer, a burly man in a navy-blue uniform, looked up from the computer screen and fastened me with one hazel eye. The other was brown. "She doesn't see visitors."

"But I'm her daughter. Tell her Evelyn is here to see her."

He repeated that Mrs Grant did not see visitors.

"But I'm her daughter." I could repeat, too. I studied one of his interesting eyes. "Tell her I'm living in our old house across the street."

But he wasn't going to tell her anything, and she wasn't going to see me. I pivoted, exited the prison, and crossed the street. Blindly I climbed the outside staircase to my empty rooms. Once inside the closet, I hit the wall with the heels of my fists and ground my forehead into the cedar. How dare she reject me!

Forty years, Evelyn. Forty years you've stayed away.

The small window high on the north wall wouldn't open. Outside, the limbs of the oak tree swayed in the wind. Shafts of late afternoon light played across the glass. I knew my mother had seen the same light from the same window when she was putting away her sewing for the day. When I was a young girl there had been no rejection. Her approval was like a sweater I could wear, throw on a chair or bed, even misplace. It was so familiar and so obviously mine that I would always find it again.

I sat down on the pile of dirty rugs and closed my eyes, listening for the hum of the sewing machine, the click of the bobbin cover. I saw in my mind's eye how a spool of thread looks when it's twirling on its spindle and suddenly stops.

Time slowed while I excavated the hum, the click, the spool on its spindle. I went over and over the sounds until they were accurate. Remembering precisely wasn't easy, but getting the past exactly right was becoming important. Paying attention was crucial. Sitting on the stack of carpeting—a mix of imitation Persian, cheap shag, a rubberized "Welcome" mat— was hard on the back and legs. There were moments when my mind wanted to stay in the closet but my body begged to get out. When begging didn't work, it tried to sleep. But I wasn't in the closet to be comfortable. I didn't allow my body much of a vote in the walk-in closet. I was here to be fully awake. This was a work-out room for remembering.

Listening hard finally paid off. I heard my mother's straight chair screech as she pushed back and stood up from the Singer sewing machine. She turned and saw me standing in the open door. She smiled while I took a little jump to use up excess energy. I ran downstairs ahead of her because I knew she'd soon be at the kitchen sink peeling potatoes and would give me a slice with a little salt. She filled the iron kettle with water and set it on the front right burner. Bending at the waist—my mother had a slim, lithe waist—she struck a match and adjusted the gas flame up, then down. She wore a house dress with a front-buttoning top, cap sleeves, and a waistband attached to a gathered skirt. Because of the buttons in front and placket at the waist, she was able to slide the dress over her head and down into place.

At her sewing machine in the closet my mother labored over darts, tucks, gores, button holes, and zippers, taming yardage into something that lies along the flesh without bunching. Undergarments further regulated: full-cut panties, sensible bra without lace, the heavy girdle with hanging garters. To attach each stocking, she deftly rolled it into a tight nest, fit it over her toes, and uncurled it up her leg all the way to the thigh where it was neatly fixed between a little wire circle and rubber button. The fastener left an imprint in her skin when she sat.

My mother's hair was dark brown and hung almost to her hips. She brushed it straight back, braided it, and arranged the braids at the nape of the neck. She plunged pronged hairpins into the coil and, like a miracle, it held, even when she turned her head. In spring, the dark hair of my mother's armpits curled beneath the cap sleeves. As the weather warmed, she cut the hair with scissors, leaning over a waste basket. Later, in summer, she shaved the hair.

In the mornings she smelled of soap. When I was in the bathroom with her, her urine smelled stronger, riper than mine. Sometimes there was blood, darkly sweet. When she dressed to go out, the scent of her face powder, flavored dust, floated ahead. Moist, flagrant lipstick smelled like candy for grown-up mouths; delicious, unsafe food; the lacquered surface of insanity.

Five

June 4th. The weather was fresh and frothy, light as a beaten egg. Earlier, Charles Glenn had helped me dislodge my windows. Now cross-breezes chased each other through the empty rooms. In a cotton skirt, blouse, and floppy hat to keep off the sun, I hurried down the outside stairs without locking the door behind me. We'd never locked the house when I was a girl and I wasn't going to start now. Anyway, unless someone wanted an inflatable mattress, card table, and two folding chairs, there was nothing to steal.

Down the street, Steve's building gleamed. The old family home that once stood on its spacious lot slept like a history lesson below the glass and steel. I turned left on Monroe. As I toiled uphill toward Miss Jaeger's piano studio, an aging Lincoln stopped in the middle of the street. Roz Teal leaned toward the passenger seat and rolled down the window.

"Going somewhere special?"

I stepped to the curb. "My old piano teacher's studio on Jackson."

The car was rolling. "Miss Jaeger used to play piano for our music appreciation club."

"You're rolling, Roz."

She stomped on the brake. "What a wonderful European background she had. I really admire cultured people." Her eyebrows lifted. "And you. Working in an art gallery. I don't know anything about art. Maybe you can teach me something. There's a watercolor exhibit down at the Community Center—"

Though she'd come to a stop, she was blocking traffic. I motioned for her to pull over. "How about a cup of tea with me this afternoon?" I said when she'd subdued the car again.

Her face created its own weather. "Love to"—sunshine. "I

need to think about something besides"— shadow, and she gestured toward the hymn-singing at the foot of the hill. "The noise is always there. It's impossible to forget the prison. Just when you think you have a moment of quiet, someone starts in on the bullhorn again. It's unbearable. I've heard every hymn a hundred times. I have a headache and a heartache. I'm used to failed appeals, but this…" She opened her purse on the seat beside her and took out a large white handkerchief. "It's too much. Too much." Sobbing—

"Are you all right to drive?" I asked.

—she buried her face in the broadcloth, shook it out, jammed it back in her bag, and waved good-bye.

"See you this afternoon," I shouted, and heard the squeal of rubber as she experimented with forward and reverse. When I turned, she was steering downhill toward Capitol.

Wearing a velvet dressing gown, and with her crimped white hair pinned close to her face, Miss Jaeger looked like what she was: a European woman born in the last century. Lame from birth, she walked with a crutch whose padded arm rest was covered in peach-colored satin. How well she'd taught classical piano, always maintaining a dignified distance between herself and the Americans she admitted into her studio. She liked us, I thought, but viewed as too casual our manners and education.

Halfway down Jackson, the old studio had deteriorated into a seedy residence whose brick looked damp from the muddy ground up. Walking toward the porch with its missing planks, I heard piano music floating from the windows. *How well did you know my mother?* I ask near the steps. The piano-playing abruptly stops. I imagine Miss Jaeger's words: *No one knew your mother. She was a mystery. Like late Beethoven.*

Sometimes Miss Jaeger played Beethoven for my mother and me on her Victrola.

"Why does she cry when she listens to records?" I would ask during the bus ride home.

"Because she's homesick. She misses Europe." My mother

would open the little assignment book. "Practice chromatic fingering," she read aloud. "Make smooth, 1-3-1-3-1-2…" When I grew drowsy on the bus, she would open her coat. The scent of lipstick and face powder, the air between her dress and coat, swirled about us as she nestled me close. I understood my parents were pleased to be raising me, not on a farm in Western Kansas where my mother had grown up, not in a small town in Idaho where my father had lived, but in a green state with rolling hills, in a capital city with fine brick and stone buildings from the previous century and a piano teacher from Europe.

Perhaps, like Miss Jaeger, my mother had been homesick. Homesick for something she never named.

I turned away and retraced my steps along Jackson, across High, back down to Capitol. By the time Roz arrived, I'd set out cups and was brewing tea in a two-person teapot purchased in town. A reverse pang of nostalgia struck: I had several lovely teapots back in Manhattan.

I suddenly missed New York and the private gallery where I worked, the crackle of artistic excitement, the thrill of chasing art and money. I missed the three rooms of paintings and sculptures. The Matisse, Cezanne, and two Maillol sculptures, carefully lighted. The Pissarro landscape with a wall to itself. The Degas charcoals, lithe trails of mineral, resting in shallow drawers of cherry wood on runners smooth as syrup.

A little to the east of my windows, a single demonstrator stood on the curb and delivered a sermon to a crowd of protestors, alternating between strident opinion and recitation of the Beatitudes. I looked down as a policeman on foot gave permission for Roz to park in front of my house. The old Lincoln bumped into the curb with a shudder. I watched her park by feel, then emerge in sections, like something hinged: head of curly hair close to the scalp; shoulder; shawl; scarf; knotted fringe at far end of shawl; lunch box; oversized pocketbook. At last, finding herself upright, Roz slammed the car door shut, barely averting a collision with a police car that had chosen a bad time to be cruising Capitol Avenue. She lumbered up the front walk. Time passed. The woman would soon be gamely climbing the outside staircase hanging off the east wall. I counted her steps and braced for a tea party.

"Snickerdoodles." She thrust the lunch box toward me. Since the only two chairs were already at the card table, I served tea without preamble. The towel appropriated for a tablecloth did not hide the flimsiness of the table or the inadequacy of the little teapot, and I feared for both as Roz seated herself and arranged her blouse and scarves.

"So did you find Miss Jaeger's studio?"

I described the run-down duplex and wondered out loud where the two grand pianos were. "Judging by the state of the building," I said, "they may have fallen through the floor."

"We have some interesting characters in town. Do you know who Professor Wolfe is? The old gentleman who carries the sign about Tiny Tim?"

"I've seen him."

"Sometimes his signs make sense, and sometimes they don't. He taught Sociology at Lincoln and developed a legal clinic to help with prisoner appeals. He worked with Tim and me. Then he got sick and had to retire." She lifted her cup. It tilted dangerously in mid-air. "His mind wanders now, but he's still committed to social justice. My ex-husband said he was the first white faculty hired after integration. He had a desk in the basement of the education building... "

She babbled on without much context since our friendship—it had begun to feel like a friendship—wasn't anchored in anything except Steve's introduction and an apparent common interest in the penitentiary. "Tiny Tim—I call him Tiny Tim—lives a few blocks from the prison"—she pointed the teacup—"on an alley that floods whenever the river rises. It's a little moldy. Couldn't be very good for his arthritis."

"What other interesting characters are there?" I asked.

"Besides you."

She smiled. "Do you know a Mrs Winthrop?" She rolled her eyes and blew her bangs upward. "The old lady yells at me all the time. She's against my literacy program. She doesn't think prisoners should learn to read at taxpayers' expense." She chugged her tea. "Tell me about Miss Jaeger's studio. I was never inside."

"There was lots of old china and photographs of German musicians," I said. "I couldn't read their signatures; they looked like spider trails on paper."

"I was never musical," Roz said. "I didn't have any reason to go to her studio. But even if I did, I don't remember what happened yesterday, much less forty years ago." A siren at the prison began to wail, then aborted.

"I lost my childhood," I said. "I guess that's why I remember so much about it. I *have* to remember or it won't have existed."

"However, I do remember all the conversations I've ever had with Tim." She put her elbows on the table, a shaky enterprise, and said confidentially, "He was abandoned by his mother. Thrown out of school after school, foster home after foster home. He's told me everything about himself, Evelyn. I remember it all." She rested her chin in her hands and whispered, "He didn't intend to kill anyone." She lifted her head. "I think a lot of people across the street didn't intend to kill." Rested her chin again. "They just don't know when they've crossed over into the unspeakable." I heard pleading behind her words. She wanted someone besides herself to love Tim Anguin.

"There but for the grace of God" was the best I could come up with. But a platitude wasn't what she was looking for. She wanted me to truly comprehend him.

"What did he do?" I asked.

She seemed uninterested in the actual crime. "He was mixed up with women." She gazed off into space. "Criminals are lacking part of themselves, Evelyn. I would talk to him about something in a law book we were reading, maybe something a judge wrote in a case on appeal, a case like his, and you could see he understood the law but not *why* there was a law. He couldn't connect it with himself." Her face gave up effort. Only sorrow remained. "I don't think he knows he's a person."

"How many of us really do?" I said casually, and lifted the lid of the teapot to inspect the water level. "How many of us understand ourselves?"

"Oh, but we do understand ourselves," she said. "We learn it early. And we learn about lawfulness early. Our mothers and fathers teach us by their eyes and by their voices." Uninterested in further shallow remarks I might offer, she stared into empty space above the card table. "What happens to us when we don't learn how to feel and behave? We're just lost forever, Evelyn. Lost. Lost."

"I like to think we can exert will power over ourselves and follow the law," I said crisply. Eager for something to do, I went into the kitchen and set the kettle boiling again. From the front room I heard Roz's chair scrape against the hardwood floor. A moment later she stood behind me.

"Every person across the street has a story," she said. "Their stories are like yours and mine and Tim's and your mother's. As real as anyone's story."

"But you and I didn't kill anyone, Roz."

She shifted her weight, and a floorboard sighed. "Have you ever been so angry that you thought you might kill someone if you didn't control yourself?"

I stooped to regulate the stuttering flame. "Maybe." There were times when, as a teenager in Idaho, my tears had turned to fury. I would never have hurt my mother, but I sometimes imagined bloodlessly getting rid of her.

"Well, there you are," Roz said. The kettle rocked unevenly as the water began to simmer. I settled it squarely over the burner. "Tim had no training," she continued. "No beliefs. No self when I first met him. He was so undeveloped that I don't think he knew what he was doing. Now he's eager to learn anything he can. He reads and listens like a starving man. But it's too late."

I turned to lay the pot holder on the counter and saw that her face was ashen. "Let's get back to the table," I said, and led her out of the kitchen. Behind us, the kettle began to rattle. In the process of seating herself, Roz knocked over her cup.

"Oh, God!" she exclaimed as cold tea splashed onto the towel. But when she leaned on the table in a clumsy attempt to right the cup in its saucer, my own cup overturned into the plate of cookies. She rolled her eyes and put her hand to her heart.

"Never mind," I said. "It doesn't matter at all. They're just cookies. It's just a card table."

"Oh," she moaned. "I'm so sorry, Evelyn. Let me wash the cloth."

"Nonsense. It's only a towel. I use the machine and dryer downstairs. No problem."

She was already moving dishes and dabbing at the table top. "Let me at least put it in to soak. Tea stains."

"I'll gather up a couple of other things," I said. The protestors in the street, whose chanting had faded from hearing, were sawing away again. I turned off the stove and gathered up laundry in the bedroom. With Roz behind me, I went down the back stairs to the washing machine and started a load.

"I guess I should go home," she said vaguely.

"Don't go yet," I said. "Let's not let a little thing like spilled tea ruin our afternoon." We sat down on the two lower steps.

"Are you alone in Jefferson City?" I asked after we'd settled ourselves. "Do you have relatives here?"

"None. I have two brothers in Pennsylvania. My parents died. I have no children. Except Tim." She fell silent. "God must have asked me to mother him."

The washer's gentle shudder, the soft gargle of the rotor, created a meditative silence. "There are probably others who need you once Tim…" I didn't finish the sentence.

"Yes. Yes. There will always be others."

"I've avoided coming home," I said.

"I still avoid coming home," Roz said, misunderstanding. "I like being out and about. I like being in town, teaching at the prison, going to one meeting or another."

"I mean I've avoided coming home to Jefferson City. I've avoided the past. Now it's all I think about."

"Are you avoiding something besides your mother's"—Roz searched for the word—"incarceration?"

"Isn't that enough?"

"For instance, why she hasn't seen you yet."

I didn't answer.

"I'm a Jew," Roz said. "But when I married Simon I started going to his church. I've stayed there. I'm a Methodist now. It reminds me of him and when we were happy. I like the congregation, and the congregation likes me. I help with Sunday School and Vacation Bible School. But some day I'll go back to the synagogue. The synagogue is home." She hugged her knees and studied the bottom step. Suddenly she looked up and fastened me in a frank, steady gaze. "I may be able to persuade your mother to see you."

The wash cycle stopped and the street noise came up like a swish of blood pressure. "How would you do that?"

"I know who she is and I know the one person in the prison she talks to. There's nothing I'd rather do than help you see your mother, especially now that—now that I won't have Tim behind the walls. I don't know about anyone else, but that's what keeps me going. Other people."

"Does the person she talks to have influence?" I said.

"Informal influence."

I appreciated her offer, but I didn't want her to meddle. My mother was not a project to keep Roz busy now that she was losing Tim. My mother was *my* mother. The spin cycle began. When the machine wobbled to a stop, I put the wet clothes in the dryer and we left by the front door of Glenn, Greenberry & Nixon.

I walked Roz to her car. Leafy trees obstructed the view of the State Capitol. I would have had to stand on the white line in the middle of the street in order to see the silver-gray dome with its tiny figure, goddess of agriculture, balanced at the top; to see the scrubbed courthouse tower and the Methodist church steeple piercing the clean air. I wished it were winter when the trees had lost their leaves and I could see, from the sidewalk, the high heart of Jefferson City silhouetted against the sky.

"Remember my offer," she said, getting into the car. I waved good-bye. On the porch I picked up the *News and Tribune* and saw a front-page article about the history of the prison. At first I averted my eyes and skipped to the editorials. The words "Missouri State Penitentiary" could still act on me like bad medicine.

Aware of my rising heartbeat, I returned to the first page and began reading about the original buildings constructed beyond city limits back before Jefferson City grew out to meet the prison. Sitting down on the top step, I focused hard on the newsprint, all but entering the grainy photographs: I criss-crossed the old yard, slipped into the broom factory and shoe factory, circled the wheat field where early hangings took place. The portraits of previous-century desperadoes were faint and specked from the old plates; several convicts in black-and-white stripes stared at the photographer who caught them in bald, goofy expressions.

A schoolmate at Moreau Heights once explained that her father worked "inside the walls." Later, just before she moved away, she said her father had gotten a job in St. Louis "outside the walls."

Patterned with ivy on the street side, the limestone wall would have looked gracious and friendly if it weren't for the razor wire and guard towers. My father told me there was no ivy growing on the other side. He told me to ignore the prison across the street and concentrate on my school work. Some people could not concentrate and could not control themselves, he said, and so the State had to do it for them. Concentration and self-control were the keys to a good life, he said. Religion is all well and good, "as your mother believes," but in the end it's safer to depend on yourself.

"What's your mother doing upstairs?" he asked me one day.

"Sewing," I lied. I knew she was praying. By now I realized the walk-in closet was no longer a sewing room. Perhaps I'd known even then that I should tell him about Mother. Perhaps if he'd known about the closet he could have done what doctors do: cure sick people.

My mother would sit, kneel, rock in the walk-in closet while I played on the floor with paper dolls. If I said, "Mother, can I do such-and-such or go play with so-and-so?" she would touch me gently and keep me with her. Sometimes I was made uneasy because she kept her eyes open without seeing anything. When I asked what she was looking at, she explained she was praying and hoped I was praying, too.

"What shall I pray for?" I asked. It was easier to pray in church where everyone prayed together; where Reverend Schmidtke would go first, where the choir would hum in the background, and where we all recited The Lord's Prayer. It was hard to pray alone with my mother, especially in what I still thought of as the sewing room. I would rather sew than pray.

"Let's put the machine up again," I said, and she slapped me, then followed the violence with tears and hugs. When she was sitting with her hands folded in her lap again, I would leave the closet and go next-door to the Pletzes'. Barbie and Jackie had a rabbit pen in the alley and we fed them vegetable peelings kept in a pail on the back porch. While my mother prayed in the closet, I got in the habit of opening the Pletzes' screen door and going on the porch without ringing the front door bell first. By myself, I would take the pail to the rabbits in the alley and watch them for hours. Mrs Pletz called and told my mother I

43

was not to go on their back porch without coming to the front door first. She said I was spending too much time alone.

"How about an ice-cream cone?" my father sometimes asked. I reached for his hand. The Masonic ring he wore on his left hand gave him ministerial weight, while his laugh up and down the bass-baritone scale produced drama. Poetry. We sang on the way to Central Dairy. He was the one who taught me to stay on tune when someone else harmonizes. My mother couldn't do it and was amazed when my father and I sang in thirds without wandering into tuneless territory.

When I was very young the three of us took rides, but as time went on, my father and I were the only ones who used the car. He still moved quickly, half-jumping into the driver's side, but it took him a while to slam the door shut. He was gaining weight.

"Thomas, you've been snacking too much," my mother would say. "You and Evelyn are eating too many sweets. Think about her teeth." But we continued to have our ice-cream cones, cherry Cokes at the Rexall counter, cheese and crackers and cookies in the kitchen. My father could still take the staircase two steps at a time, but his footfall was heavier when he landed, and he breathed loudly at the top.

"I walk miles when I'm on hospital rounds," he would say to Mother. "You don't realize how much walking I do." But still he gained weight. I didn't mind. To me, he was a giant of good humor and musicality, a Scottish Rite Mason who attended important meetings in the stone Masonic Hall with fluted pillars and a hundred steps that he would always be able to take two at a time.

My father, stuffing himself with sweets, believed in self-control; my mother, serving a life sentence in prison, believed in prayer. Pray for the prisoners, she said, because they've made mistakes and we all need to be forgiven for our sins. And so I prayed for the prisoners, and threw in Catholics and Negroes for good measure. In Jefferson City you were either white or Negro, Catholic or Protestant, inside or outside the walls.

I put down the newspaper and stared across the street at the limestone wall warming itself in the afternoon sun. As a girl, I'd imagined a prisoner climbing over the top at midnight, in the moonlight, one leg over the wall, then the other. He runs, half-bent, across the street, sneaks in the basement door, and kidnaps my pretend little sister. At this point I come running down the stairs shouting for help. With his prey slung over his shoulder—my imaginary sister in a gunny sack, her head bouncing against his kidneys—the bad man runs out the front door and into the arms of the police.

Watching the sunlight crawl along the wall until twilight rendered everything silver-gray and luminous, I wished a little girl from the neighborhood would wander by with a set of jacks. I still admired and coveted ten shiny jacks and a clean, white ping-pong ball. I knew exactly how a cool porch feels when you've hiked up your dress and wrapped your legs around a game. You don't want a rough surface to distort the bounce of the perfectly light, crisp ball.

Steve Mason pulled up at the curb, got out of his car, and came up the front walk. He left the motor running.

"How's it going?"

I shook my head. I must have looked pathetic.

"Wait while I turn off the engine." He came back and sat down. "What's the matter?" Sitting on porch steps erased the years. We might have been in fourth grade again.

"My husband died," I answered truthfully. "My children live in California. I feel this pull from Missouri, but I don't know where I belong." I didn't mention my mother.

"I think I know what you mean."

"With all due respect, Steve, I doubt it. You've lived in one place all these years."

He didn't agree or disagree.

"I mean, it must be soothing to live in the same town all

your life."

"You'd think so."

From the locust trees that surrounded Glenn, Greenberry & Nixon, mourning doves stroked the oncoming twilight with their velvety gray calls.

"How long do doves live?" I asked.

"I have no idea."

The birds I was hearing could be the great-great-great-great-grandbirds of the doves who had cooed when I was a girl.

"How about a trip to the mall?" he asked.

Buying something would not make me feel better. Still, I didn't want to be alone, so we got in the car and drove through city streets toward the highway. On the way, we passed Moreau Heights, our dignified, two-story grade school, focus of the centennial celebration.

"Beautiful old building, isn't it?" He studied it serenely through the windshield. Glancing over at me he said, "So what are you going to buy?"

I couldn't think of anything I wanted. "A magazine."

"Big-time spender. How about some new shoes?"

"Keep my feet on the ground?"

"Sure. Maybe I'll get some, myself."

I sat reading on a bench just inside the entrance to the mall. Steve came back to where I sat, wearing new loafers that already looked comfortable. Glancing without interest at the cover of my *New Yorker*, he pointed to an ice-cream cart parked on the far side of the blue pool with its thundering, overwrought fountain and said, "What's your flavor?" Morosely, I watched him stroll toward the line of retail carts plodding through the mall.

"How often do you come here, Steve?" I asked when he returned with two chocolate cones.

"Whenever I need to buy something."

I think my smile was slightly superior.

"Hold on there a minute," he said. "We have twenty-two restaurants in this mall. That includes the food court. And in winter," he added, "it's warm. In summer it's cool." We sat side by side on the bench, eating our ice-cream, watching shoppers glide by in slow motion.

"Plans all made for the reunion?" I asked.

He examined his ice-cream. "The execution has thrown us a curve ball."

A reflex prayer learned from my mother flew through my mind. Dear Lord, bless Tim Anguin.

"It will all be over by the time the reunion starts," I said.

"It's hard to shake off," he said. "We've already had some cancellations."

"I'll admit I don't feel much like celebrating."

He looked in my direction but not actually at me. "I guess you've come to see your mother—"

"Yes."

"—more than for the reunion." He looked hurt.

"We all owe you and Roz a debt of gratitude for putting the event together," I said.

"Roz isn't as interested as she was. Tim Anguin took care of that."

"Without the reunion, I would have put off coming back to Jeff City even longer," I said.

"Have you been putting it off?"

"Only forty years."

"And have you seen your mother?"

I shook my head.

"This Tim Anguin business makes it hard on everyone."

"Especially Tim Anguin."

"He should have thought of that before he did what he did," Steve said. He looked at me sideways. "How do you feel about capital punishment?"

"Some things deserve severe punishment," I said. "Whether death, I don't know."

He started to comment, but stopped himself. He'd suddenly remembered my mother.

"Roz is devastated," I said. "Some people can claim insanity and avoid execution, but Tim can't."

Steve tilted his head at a ruminative angle. "After this is all over," he said, "you might talk to Roz about your mother."

"Why?"

"Well, she knows the prison inside and out. She probably knows about your mother. Might even know her."

"What do *you* know about my mother?" I asked. "You're familiar with the prison, too."

"I know very little about her." He looked uncomfortable.

"Do you know anything at all?"

"She's the only woman left behind the walls. One thing I do know: she doesn't bother anyone and she doesn't want anyone to bother her." He stood.

I stood, too. "And why is she the only woman left in the prison?"

"Well," he said, "she was the X-ray technician. And she got older and older, and …"

"Couldn't they train a male?"

We began walking. "Someone with influence wanted her there."

"My father?"

Steve shrugged. "That, too. Ask Roz. She'll be able to tell you anything you want to know."

The streetlights outside the entrance had attracted moths. Here on the asphalt in front of the mall, an unlikely spot, I was surprised by a moment of strange, intense happiness. Forty years earlier Steve and I would have been playing tag in a vacant lot, or catching fireflies in jars. As a girl I'd experienced this weather, this climate, before. I'd loved being alive. I'd loved the fulsome Missouri nights and my parents and friends and the fireflies. I still did.

On the way back to Capitol Avenue we passed our old grade school again.

"Let's look around," I said impulsively. He parked the car on the street and we entered the Moreau Heights grounds.

The school had been abandoned years ago. Windows aligned in the red brick façade reflected an occasional passing headlight, then went dark. Night scent of honeysuckle transformed ordinary air into a single balmy evening that summarized June nights.

A piece of gravel in my sandal rolled from toe to heel as I followed Steve past the outside fire escape, a metal tube constructed to funnel children from a hypothetical burning schoolhouse and empty them onto the playground. Farther on, he gave the merry-go-round a push—it resisted with a shriek—and ambled toward the swings. In the corner by the fence we sat on the board seats. Swaying a little back and forth, he kept one foot on the ground and turned toward me.

"I've got the damndest situation in one of my apartments," he said. "I've got a mystery woman for a renter." He stopped and gathered steam for a story. "She rented my first-floor studio last January. She's a waitress at the hotel. Charlie Johnson—you probably remember Charlie, he was two classes behind us—he owns the hotel and says she does a good job for him. I never have to ask her for the rent. She pays on the 1st like clockwork."

"How old is she?"

"Young. Maybe twenty. Maybe younger. Attractive, but always looks"—he pushed himself in another back-and-forth motion—"tired."

"She lives alone?"

"Yep. I've never seen any visitors. Of course, I'm not there all the time."

"Do you do all the maintenance on your building yourself?"

"I'm not a busy guy. Might as well. Save myself money."

"Everything? The heating, electricity, roof?"

"Several of us who have buildings in town help each other

out. For instance, Ron Hill—you remember Ron, he was in the class ahead of us. He's an electrician, so if I have a problem I'll call him." He took hold of the swing chain. "Yeah, so she's a good tenant. Charlie over at the hotel doesn't know where she's from. She's not from around here." He shifted on the swing seat and reached higher up on the chain. "So one day while I'm at the building mowing the lawn, this pickup truck pulls over to the curb and parks. A burly guy in overalls gets out of the truck and comes up to me. 'You the landlord here?' he asks.

"'That's me.' I give him my name. He doesn't tell me his.

"'I've got something here for one of your renters.'

"'Who's that?' I say.

"'The gal in the ground-floor studio.'

"'What have you got?'

"'An ice-box.'

"'Well, there's already a refrigerator in that unit,' I say.

"'This is for her to keep. Her mother and me don't need it.'

"'Are you her father?'

"He nods. I turn off the mower and unlock the studio. She's left the curtains drawn. It's dark and looks kind of unlived-in. He carries it in—it's a small refrigerator, just for one person—looks around once, and leaves like he wants to get away. Outside, he shakes my hand. Gives me a look. 'Don't tell her I was here.'

"'She'll know someone was here,' I say. 'That refrigerator didn't walk in by itself.'

"He shrugs. 'Tell her whatever you want.' And he goes back to the truck. Just before he gets in he says, 'She don't talk to us no more.'"

In the overgrown shrubs behind us a night bird rustled.

"I wave, he drives away, and I finish mowing the lawn."

"Is that it?" I said. "Is that the story?"

The moon was high enough now to show above the roof of the school. My mother and I swung here once. We'd tried to keep our swings in rhythm. She said we weighed different amounts and that was the reason we kept falling out of synch. She said there was probably a mathematical equation for our weight, speed of swinging, height of the seat, and maybe some other things, too. She lost a hairpin while she was swinging and laughed when her hair came loose. Her hair blew behind her, then fell forward, fell back, fell forward.

Fascinated by my mother pumping herself higher and higher in a swing, by her undone hair, by her knowledge, I asked what a mathematical equation was. She said it was a clever way to express facts, like a swing moving through the air and how different people sitting in it could affect how fast and how high it flew. I remembered another of her statements: "'God is no-where' really spells 'God is now-here.'" But immediately her face had turned blank and private. "God will reveal to you everything you need to know, Evelyn."

Steve hadn't finished his story. "So I went back to lock up the studio and looked around the room, probably more than I should have. I opened the door of the refrigerator her father had brought. It was empty. I looked around some more. I didn't touch anything"—he paused while a motorcycle roared by on the other side of the chain link fence—"until I saw some pictures hanging above the table. Religious pictures."

"What kind of religious pictures?"

"Oh, some were homemade pencil drawings. Some might have been a Christmas card or something. The head of Jesus. In color, you know."

I was tired of this non-story about a girl who had non-taste in art and was on the outs with her family. My mother was far more interesting. I got off the swing. It moved behind me, bobbing, wobbling, until it fell into its own rhythm. Steve stood, too, and held the chain of his swing, studying the ragged motion. When it settled into a smooth sway again, he began walking. I followed him past the teeter-totters and jungle gym.

"I turned one of the pictures of Jesus over," he said, starting the car and pulling away from the curb. "There was an article about Tim Anguin. I turned over all the pictures. On the backs were newspaper articles about the guy."

"About his crime?"

"The crimes, the trial, the penitentiary."

"Poor girl," I said. "Maybe he's her brother."

"Maybe."

"Did you ever ask her?"

He turned full-face and said, "I'm her landlord. If she wants to tell me, fine. I don't pry."

He noticed my silence.

"Usually I don't pry." He smiled a little and looked at me with colorless but observant eyes that hadn't missed much when he was a boy. "A landlord has to know what's going on inside his property."

"You still don't know," I said.

"No, I still don't know."

We approached Capitol Avenue. The protestors were unusually silent this evening, perhaps saving their voices for the various Sunday services throughout town the next morning. Steve parked in a carport behind his building and walked me back up Monroe, onto Capitol, and to my apartment.

"I suppose things will get more hectic the closer we are to Wednesday," I said.

"Count on it."

"Won't everything calm down after that?" I said. "Won't the school reunion go as planned? Won't all this be behind us?"

He didn't answer until we'd passed a ragged group of sign-bearers.

"The town doesn't forget easily," he said. "A public death affects everyone. Children are upset. Everyone's over-stimulated." We'd reached Glenn, Greenberry & Nixon and stood at the foot of my staircase. "I'll say good-night now. Family duty calls. An uncle of mine. He's in the nursing home. I visit him every Saturday."

I looked at my watch. "It's late."

"Oh, I've already seen him today. It's his paperwork and bills I have to work on."

Across the street, search lights rotated above the prison yard. My mother was probably getting ready for bed.

"Do you pay for his expenses?" I asked.

"No, he's got money. I just write the checks. But he's also got a daughter. She thinks I'm stealing from him." The search light caught us and set his eyeglass lenses on fire. "She's threatening to get a lawyer." Mocking himself, he tipped his head toward the prison. "I may be over there some day." But he couldn't hide bitterness.

I touched his arm, tense as cable. "Why doesn't his daughter manage his affairs?"

"He doesn't trust her." He gave me the semblance of a hug, one arm, shoulder to shoulder. "See you around the neighborhood." I watched him cross the street and enter his building.

Upstairs, from my half-open window, I could make out the heads and shoulders of the guards in the towers. Floodlights would be criss-crossing the prison yard all night, held in synch for a few sweeps before falling out of rhythm again, rolling east, rolling west, large eyes set too close together, then too far apart.

I went back outside to the landing. The moon, a few nights away from being full, hung above the wall, lop-sided and pale. Across the alley behind me, the upstairs windows of the Anderson house were brightly lit. I tried to remember which bedroom had been the babies'. Mentally I tried entering the nursery that day... smelling the powdered creases in their little necks... hearing my mother's breaths and the movements of her skirt...

As a girl, I'd been more interested in Mrs Anderson's pregnancy than in the twin boys she'd delivered. I'd watched the woman's swelling belly and paid attention to her maternity clothes, how the jacket fell, rounded and shapeless, over the mysterious sexual region where babies, with the help of their fathers, get inside their mothers, then get out again.

Had my mother crossed the packed dirt and entered the Anderson house through the kitchen? Had she skirted the garage and gone in through the side door? Had she been praying in the sewing room/chapel? Or had she merely been washing dishes? Was her hair combed, or flying wild and loose?

I snagged myself on the blistered gray railing. Palm up, I began removing sharp paint flecks and a splinter. Standing there picking at the inside of my hand, I stared at the prison wall across the street, laboring to make my mother innocent; trying to secrete pearl around the gritty fact of a double bathtub drowning.

I wanted to hear hymn-singing: it masked my despair. Descending to the street, I walked west, stepping behind protestors who were sitting on the curb, maneuvering around sleeping bags being unrolled at edges of lawns. On the opposite side, lights burned in Steve's building. A door on the ground floor opened, and in the illumination thrown up by outdoor lighting anchored in the flowerbed, a young woman stepped through the door and locked it behind her.

I guessed immediately it was Steve's tenant. Her high heels tapped prettily, carrying her through a dark zone between the yard and the sidewalk. When she emerged from the shadows into the street light, she looked as if she were dressed for church. A Saturday night service, perhaps. I had to squint in order to bring into focus the sundress with wide straps and modest neckline, the dark hair done in a single braid. The braid hung over one shoulder and bounced against the bodice of her dress. She turned right at the corner, apparently to get her car, because a minute or two later she came driving up Monroe. I'd expected a clunker, grinding gears, black smoke, a loose tailpipe. But she moved smoothly up the hill toward town, headlights cutting brightly through the night.

As I turned around and walked back toward the lawyers' offices where I rented a second-floor apartment in a town where I no longer belonged, I wished I were a pretty young woman with one lustrous braid bouncing against my breast, high heels clicking on the sidewalk, a street lamp shining on my face, a church service to attend, a God to believe in, a mother and father still alive. I hoped the young woman would end the impasse with her parents and speak to them. I imagined her calling them up in some backwoods town where they lived.

"Thank you for the refrigerator," she would say. "It was nice of you to bring it to Jeff City. I wish I'd been here to see you. I'll be home for a visit next week…"

However, I didn't want to be a young woman with a brother or boyfriend on death row. It was bad enough being a fifty-year-old with a mother serving a life sentence. And then I thought perhaps there was not so much difference between us after all, except that the girl probably visited Tim Anguin as often as she could and was not turned away. And the fact, of course, that he was going to die on Wednesday.

Six

"Do you know if he's her brother? Her boyfriend?" I asked Steve the next day as we drove toward his farm west of town.

He'd seen me walking early Sunday morning and asked if I'd like to ride out to the country with him. He didn't actually grow anything, he told me, but kept himself busy making repairs on the farmhouse. He'd put a new roof on the barn with the help of his son. Mainly he used the sixty acres, wooded and overgrown with brush, for hunting deer and wild turkey. On a tour of the house I saw in one of the upstairs bedrooms—small rooms built before the Civil War, with slanted ceilings and shallow closets—a number of bright orange vests hanging from hooks on the wall.

"For hunting," he said. There were several pairs of boots. A bunch of wild turkey feathers lay on a table. The farmhouse smelled slightly moldy from being closed up.

In the pickup truck he hadn't satisfactorily answered my question about the mystery woman, preferring to point out features of the landscape. "See that tree stump split by lightning? A creek runs right behind it. You'll almost always find deer there. And over here"—he slowed and pointed to a wooded hill a mile or two away—"you can still find cougars."

"Cougars!"

"Oh, there's wildcat in these woods. You won't see them often, but they're here."

Seated at the round oak table in the dining room, he opened a thermos of iced tea and said, as if he hadn't been talking about deer, cougars, fescue grass, webworms, "I don't know what my tenant is to Tim Anguin. Girl friend, friend, sister. Hell, cousin. But I know she visits him. I fish with some of the Corrections guys and they've told me so. They say she's quieted him down considerably."

"Was he—"

"A wild man. Solitary lockup."

Through the open doors of the house, front and back, I could hear birds call to each other from tree to tree. Quick-eyed, Steve moved to one of the narrow old windows and pointed to an oak. "See the cardinal?" We watched the redbird move his head in tiny, quick adjustments. His lively eye, a shiny black chip, made every other animated object in the world seem sluggish. He flew off, a bright red slash through the trees.

Back at the table, Steve poured my tea into a plastic glass and drank his from the cap.

"What did you do when you worked in the prison?" I asked.

"Kept a sharp lookout over one shoulder." He gave the thermos a couple of turns. "Made repairs on buildings. Drew plans for renovations. Supervised construction projects. There was equipment in the hospital that had to be worked on. I was what they call a square man. A non-inmate behind the wall."

It was hot in the old farmhouse. We carried our tea out to the front porch that caught an occasional breeze. The house sat on a narrow but steep hill. When we came out the front door we looked almost straight down at the barn on the right. Venerable old maples and oaks shaded the yard. In back, an outhouse stood at a distance. His son had cut a half moon into the door. Steve was proud of that half moon: it gave a comic-strip look, a touch of hillbilly humor, to the place.

We sat on the porch bench and leaned against the siding. Behind us, in the living room, he'd shown me the original logs of the cabin that formed the core of the house. He'd left them where they were and refused to paint over them. The cabin had been built around 1840, he said.

I wondered if there were any battlefield sites nearby. I'd read about the Missouri Compromise and, later, bloody skirmishes during the war, outright battles. "Miz-zer-ruh"—I still pronounced it the way we'd said it when we were growing up—

had been a slave state. The Free-Staters lived mostly in towns. People out here in the country had probably been Southern sympathizers.

Now, instead of musket shots, crickets pulsed in the grass and a buzzard spread its wings above the barn. In a tree near the house, a squirrel rasped noisily as it fed.

"I saw your mystery tenant the other night," I said.

"Oh?"

"Not very clearly. It was dark. She was coming out of her apartment."

"She's up on her rent."

"It was Sunday night and she was nicely dressed."

"Uh-huh."

"She might have been going to church. An evening service."

"She might have been going to a bar."

"I thought, with all the religious pictures—"

"Don't forget the newspaper articles on the backs of those pictures. She and Anguin have been to plenty of bars." He watched the buzzard land on the roof of the barn and spread its enormous wings. "Do you know why buzzards do that? To get warm. They absorb the heat through their wing spread."

"It must feel good to have the farm and know so much about nature."

"I've never thought much about the things I know," he said. "I just grew up knowing them. I've always preferred the out-of-doors."

"The out-of-doors isn't as complicated as the indoors."

"You can say that again. Not as mean, either. Not as disappointing."

"I can imagine," I said automatically.

"With all due respect, Evelyn, I doubt it."

I sat up straight on the bench. "With a mother in prison you don't think I understand meanness and disappointment?"

He lapsed into silent cynicism, a quality I didn't associate with the boy Steve Mason. "Try working there for a living."

I conceded the topic.

"We're calling the reunion off."

"Because of the execution?"

He walked to the edge of the porch and emptied a few last drops of tea into the bushes. "Yeah. We'll reschedule it for the fall. The weather will be cooler then. Roz agrees with me. The response isn't what we'd hoped." He was staring at the bushes but looking inward. "Most people have more important things to do than celebrate their grade school."

"My childhood is all-important to me," I assured him. "I wish it were less important. I actually can't forget it."

He looked down at me. "You said yourself you don't feel like celebrating."

"I'm here, aren't I? I wouldn't be here if I hadn't gotten your letter. Your hard work hasn't panned out right now," I said, "but it will." I stood up from the bench. "And as far as your uncle's business affairs go, Steve, you're an honest man. Everyone knows that."

"You think?"

"Of course."

"My cousin's never forgiven me," he said. "She's getting even. But I do know I'm honest."

"Forgiven you for what?"

For a moment I thought he was going to tell me. "It's a long story," he said.

"How long have you been divorced?"

"Not long enough," he said. "It was a bad marriage. It's funny, isn't it, how some people want you to stay married at all costs." I started to offer a standard response—*oh, I wouldn't know, my marriage was such a good marriage, perfect, in fact,* etc., but his bland, hazel-gray eyes had turned greenish and stormy, too stormy for clichés.

"Some people shouldn't stay married," I agreed. But I didn't try to leverage my remark into conversation because Steve had lapsed into a silence that contained depths of resentment. We hadn't escaped the mood on Capital Avenue after all. I pictured the sentimental images of Jesus hanging on his mystery tenant's walls and bulletin board, the rainbows, the sunrises, artistically dreadful renderings in contrast to the fine art of, say, my place of employment, the Manhattan gallery where some of the finest work of the nineteenth century hung at elbow-, shoulder-, eye-level, all catalogued and skillfully illuminated

I must hurry back to New York, I thought. I must hurry back to Cezanne and Matisse and Degas and showings and catalogs and lunches with buyers and sellers.

But I was capable of loving bad art, too. The stained-glass windows in First Methodist were of inferior quality, the colors weak, the representations imitative. Why was I fond of them? Why did I love the crudely done Jesus who hovered above stiff lambs?

My mother's faith—not abstract or artistic or intellectual but personal enough for her to want Jesus in her sewing room—embarrassed me. So transparently childish. Jesus, himself, embarrassed me, sentimentalized by the ages. Still, in church I felt a nostalgic longing for my mother's Jesus. Where did that homesickness, Jesus-sickness, come from?

Steve stirred out of his dark preoccupation.

"My parents came from a long line of Christians," I said in a burst of irrelevance. "They followed rules."

"Is that so?"

Do unto others as you would have others do unto you. Love thy neighbor as thyself. Thou shalt have no other Gods before me. God helps those who help themselves. A rolling stone gathers no moss. A whistling girl and a crowing hen will always come to some bad end.

"My parents didn't smoke or drink," I added.

Steve's eyes were grayish-hazel again. Undistinguished. He'd recovered from his grim silence and was warily following my disjointed trail. He studied me for a minute, took a swallow of iced tea, then turned to watch a vulture that had begun floating high above the barn. "I thought your dad smoked." His tone was as lazy as the bird's circles, but I knew he was disagreeing with me.

"I never saw him smoke," I said defensively, and felt deeply uneasy, as if my father were sitting right there beside us, smoking.

"I remember him smoking after a school program," Steve said. "My parents and I left by the front gate. He was standing east of the steps, smoking under the maple."

Offended, I carried my glass into the kitchen and rinsed it in a bucket on the drain board. On the other side of the room was a tin sink with a pump handle, though Steve said the cistern had been abandoned long ago and cemented over. Water was stored in bottles on the closed-in porch called the mudroom where hunters removed their boots and leaned their rifles in the wainscoted corners.

He broke into my thoughts. "I didn't upset you, did I?"

"Well, yeah, you did."

He went upstairs. I heard him closing windows. When he returned to the ground floor he said, "You don't want me to say something I don't mean, do you?"

"I sure do." We didn't talk much on the drive back to town. Our silence had sediment in it. My thoughts jumped from the wooded hills to a mental image of my father driving through town one afternoon in the fifties. I'd been alone at the bus stop near Miss Jaeger's studio when I saw his Hudson go by. He was singing. His bass voice, beautiful, solid, expressive, enchanted me. Before I could call out to him, I saw a cigarette in his hand. His arm was out the window and he was tapping ash into the street. I jumped behind a lilac bush. I knew I was not supposed to see the cigarette. Even more, I knew I wasn't supposed to tell my mother.

If I, a child, knew he smoked, my mother certainly knew. If a casual observer, a little boy like Steve Mason, knew, then everyone knew. And if everyone, including myself, knew, why had I forgotten? And now having remembered, why was I defending him all these years later as a man who didn't smoke? And why had I been taught that Jesus despised cigarettes? Why had my parents pretended that Jesus wasn't looking when my father smoked? Did they see the cigarette themselves? Did they see each other?

"My parents weren't perfect but they were very good." I felt narrow, prissy, and inaccurate. Steve looked at me sideways. The landscape on both sides of the road deteriorated. The green drained out of trees. I wondered why I was injecting my parents into the afternoon at the farm; why the past constantly overpowered the present. I wondered why I couldn't simply enjoy an outing with a friend, in the present tense.

Steve kept one hand on the gearshift, ready to change speed and direction. When he began to talk about how the Lewis and Clark expedition had camped nearby, I realized I could not keep up with his brisk travel between himself and the world; between the past and the present.

"Well," Roz said early that same afternoon, looking about my empty room, "you're still a minimalist."

"Did you expect me to furnish the apartment since the last time you were here? Which was yesterday, I believe." She'd warned me she didn't like to stay at home and I was beginning to believe it. "My furniture and paintings are in New York."

"Since you work in an art gallery, you must know a lot about art."

"I know some things about art."

"I envy you. I lack a certain... cultural polish." She scrutinized the blank walls as if there were something hanging there she couldn't see. Giving up the search, she threw velvet-and-brocade over one shoulder, sat down at the card table, and said out of the blue, "The anthem at church this morning was lovely."

"My father used to sing solos at church. He had a wonderful bass voice." My tone sounded argumentative. I went to the kitchen and pulled two glasses from the bare cupboard and a pitcher of iced tea from the refrigerator. "But yes," I said, back at the card table, "I'm sure it was a nice anthem this morning."

"Do you have any lemon?"

I got up again, careful not to hit the card table leg, and returned with lemon slices and sugar. Transferring, spoonful by spoonful, a vast quantity of sugar into her glass, she began talking. "After my divorce I considered moving away. I was heartsick. But my friends were here. I was teaching. I got the house when we split up, so I had a place to live. I've almost paid it off." She looked up from the sugaring operation. "You poor kid. These empty rooms… " She gestured with her spoon and left the sentence unfinished.

"Wow, that's a lot of sugar, Roz."

"If I stir, it will be too sweet." Sitting heavily on the folding chair, she was a physical slug but a peppy talker. "When are you going back to New York?"

"I'm not sure. I miss Manhattan. I miss my husband."

"Your husband died," she said. "He's not there anymore."

"I mean I'm at loose ends. To be frank, I'm a wreck."

She tasted her tea and added lemon.

"His death brought up some earlier trauma," I confided without actually confiding. The vocabulary wasn't mine. When the children came for their father's funeral, I'd told them I was homesick beyond words. They suggested I come to Jefferson City. I needed reconciliation with my past, they said. I needed closure. They used words like "trauma" and "avoidance." They were careful not to mention my mother; their grandmother.

Roz carefully lifted the glass of iced tea to her lips without disturbing the sugar at the bottom. "Without projects," she added, "I would have fallen apart long ago. Would you like to have a project while you're here?"

"What kind of project?"

"Oh, I don't know. Work. Volunteer. Get a life, as they say."

I looked into my glass. "I had a life before my husband died."

"Do you sew?"

I shook my head.

"Because I belong to a sewing circle. We meet once a week and knit, embroider, and crochet items for the nursing home." She stopped. "No? Okay. How about a reading circle? We meet every month and discuss a book. We also read to the blind."

I shook my head again.

"No? Okay. How about our Bible class at the church? We meet every other Sunday evening; in fact, we're meeting tonight. We're up to Deuteronomy. The Pentateuch," she said knowledgeably. "Our minister leads the reading and discussion."

"I don't believe in God and Jesus."

"No? Okay. How about my political action group? We—"

"No."

"How about volunteering at the prison?" Both of us looked out the window at the penitentiary across the street. Rather, at the wall, since we couldn't actually see beyond it and the administration building; the prison itself was sunk in a kind of quarry where inmates over the years had dug out rock for construction material.

"My mother used to tell me to pray for the prisoners," I said.

"Well, you can't pray for them if you don't believe in God."

I resented the logic. "Maybe I can't pray to God and Jesus," I said mysteriously, "but I can still—"

"Still what?"

"—pray to"—I tried to name the thing I worshipped—"Our Lady of Nostalgia."

"Oh," Roz said, as if she'd missed hearing about this interesting deity. "Who's that?"

It was my mother. It was myself, now composed mostly of memory. I was worshipping myself.

Other women lose their husbands without reverting to childhood. I hated myself for trying to be a child again. I resented my mother for ruining lives; my father for taking me away from Jefferson City and leaving me with his parents, their clothes smelling of mothballs, their sensible shoes an embarrassment. I even resented my husband. If he'd watched where he was walking, he wouldn't have been hit by a truck. Then I hated myself all over again for being unfair. No one had asked me to rent the second floor of my childhood home, to be in a position of a despairing little girl needing to be propped up by this woman sitting across the table from me, a totemic woman who might lack a family in the usual sense of the word but whose clan, tribe, nation was made up of multifarious circles for helping others. A woman who wore velvet in summer. A lumbering figure who never stayed home because she had a meeting twice every day for this or that.

"Tell me about volunteering at the prison," I said.

"Well, we have a literacy program." She leaned back in her chair. "In fact, you're looking at it."

So that's what a literacy program looked like.

"I can use some help. You can be my apprentice. My assistant. My—under-teacher."

Having never been anything but a mediocre student, I was definitely an under-teacher. The prisoners deserved better. "What would I be doing in the literacy program?"

"Bring me some more tea, please, Evelyn."

I went into the kitchen. When I'd returned and reseated myself, a shadow cast by the warden's ornate Victorian house at the corner had begun to form on the limestone wall.

"I can't teach anyone anything," I said, keeping my eyes on the shadow.

Roz touched my shoulder. "No?" she said gently. "Okay. We'll find something else for you to do. In the meantime, finish your tea. Come for supper tonight. My house. Split-pea soup. We'll talk a little. You don't have to come home until you're good and ready."

"I don't know where my home is."

Roz took a swig of tea and set down the glass. "Be a turtle. Carry your home with you."

The elementary nugget of wisdom irritated me. It sounded like something one would say to a preschooler.

"We'll have our soup and talk," Roz repeated, as if soothing a fretful child. She departed from her usual practice and carried our glasses to the kitchen. Returning, she picked up her purse from the floor. "I have some understanding of what you're dealing with." At the screen door she hitched the bag over her shoulder. "I know quite a lot about your mother."

I rose up out of my chair, and motioned for her to sit again. She came back, pulled the folding chair out from under the table, and once again lowered herself onto its seat. Carefully lining up her black Oxfords, toe to toe, heel to heel, she lifted her head. Her broad face was as open as custard but with a troubling film; milky, glossy, slightly dimpled with—was it sympathy? Pride in knowing more about my mother than I did?

"I asked at the prison about you," she said. Her scarves and shawl had loosened. "I'm friends with someone who knows your mother."

"Who's that?"

"An inmate. A trusty. He helps in the literacy program."

I wished I could chat like a normal person about my mother: how is she these days? What do you hear of her? Is she well? How does she occupy herself?

Instead I blurted out, "Does she ever mention me?"

"I don't know. I haven't ever talked to her." The milky surface of Roz's face quivered, wind across pudding. She looked back down at the shoe clumps. The folding chair squeaked.

"I'm here because of my mother," I said, "but my mother doesn't want to see me."

She hooked the heels of her Oxfords on the metal rung of

the chair. "Come help me with the class. I'm sure we can fix up some kind of meeting. The prison is lax right now. It's almost empty. The rules are broken left and right. I'm friends with the guards." Her skirt had risen. I averted my eyes from her calves and knees. I didn't want this woman to fix up a meeting. I shouldn't have to be fixed up with my mother like some blind date.

"I'm afraid I can't help you with the class," I said.

Roz stood a second time. "No?" She touched me on the shoulder. "Come for supper. Six-thirty?"

I was ashamed of my hunger pang. I would have one meal with Roz, and then stop seeing the woman. I wanted to meet my mother without anyone's interference.

Seven

I awoke from a woolly afternoon nap to cool rain splashing against the windows. While I'd slept, the weather had changed. Leaves of the locust trees rattled each time wind sighed around the corner of the house. Loneliness seeped through me, not like rain going down into a lawn, but water rising from an underground pool. One lone automobile, a lawyer working on Sunday afternoon, rolled silently along the wet driveway into the paved lot at the back of the yard. Unlike week days, there was no aroma of coffee filtering up through the floorboards; no snatches of conversation rising from offices.

I had a couple of hours before Roz's split-pea soup. I got to my feet, gathered up my shoulder bag and umbrella, and left the apartment. At the sidewalk I turned west and faced into the rain. Minutes later, I found myself inside the Methodist Church. I'd just finished a tour through Sunday School rooms, Fellowship Hall, the church kitchen where my mother had helped serve prayer breakfasts, all quiet after their Sunday morning workout, when the street door to Capitol Avenue opened. Roz crossed the threshold carrying a stack of books and roll of rain-spattered butcher paper.

"Hi," she said, as if she'd been expecting me. "We're enrolling kids for Vacation Bible School this afternoon. Can you help me with this stuff?"

I took the roll of paper and followed her to a large Sunday School room where rows of child-sized chairs waited with a patient formality that would always, sooner or later, be disturbed by squirming bodies. A piano angled out from one corner.

With a smack Roz dropped the books onto a tabletop and threw one end of her shawl over her shoulder. "We're supposed to start at 4:00, but frankly, I don't see how we'll be ready. The other teacher has an emergency." She paused. "Can you help? It's only for an hour. I'm doing a short opening lesson."

"Oh, no," I said. "I'm not prepared."

"Just as you are, Evelyn."

The line of a hymn went through my mind: *"Just as I am, thine own to be."* The melody rose to the second and last lines: *"Friend of the young, who lovest me, To consecrate myself to thee, O Jesus Christ!"* It was yearning that needed a target, and that target was Jesus. My mother must have been uttering a similar cry—*"My life to give, my vows to pay, with no reserve and no delay!"*—when she'd turned the sewing closet into a chapel.

A pang of regret immobilized me. What had my mother lacked that my father and I should have provided? *"I would live ever in the light... Just as I am, young, strong and free, to be the best that I can be..."* I looked at two children who wandered in. Their mothers hugged them, waved from the doorway, and left.

"Well, what would I be doing?"

"Can you play the piano?"

"I haven't played in years. Not since my own children were little. I'm not here to... to—"

"To live in the present?" Roz's voice tightened. "Fine. I'll handle this myself."

I forced myself toward the piano, rolled back the lid, and studied the keyboard. Still standing, I attempted a scale. Miss Jaeger, where are you, now that I need you? A stack of bright red hymnals was on top of the old upright. I picked one up, opened it to the index of first lines, and found "Just as I am." I sat down on the piano stool and began playing while Roz laid a workbook and hymnal on each chair. Children straggled in. While the older ones helped distribute enrollment cards, Roz went down the hall to the kitchen and began rattling trays and glasses. A boy of about eight passed out bookmarks in the shape of a cross to the children who were now milling about. I stood, gave the piano stool a couple of spins, and sat back down to face them.

"Good afternoon." One or two returned the greeting. The

others stared. It had been a long time since I'd spoken more than a few words to a child. The young families in our New York apartment building were self-contained. People spoke very little in the elevators.

"Do you have a favorite song?"

"Rudolph the Red-Nosed Reindeer," a little blonde girl with pure blue pools for eyes answered.

Someone snickered. "It's not Christmas!"

"Never mind." I motioned for the child to come stand beside me. I began picking out chords for "Rudolph." Now the little girl realized all too well it wasn't Christmas. She reached for the keyboard and stilled my hands. I pulled the child onto my lap and began to play *"Jesus loves me, this I know, 'cause the Bible tells me so."*

More snickers. "That's a baby song!"

The little girl stilled my hands again and twisted to look up into my face. *"Oh, say, can you see,"* she said, and began to sing the national anthem quietly and off-key.

"I don't know how to play that," I said. "How about—" and I picked out "America the Beautiful." A few of the older children knew the words and began to sing under their breaths. The blue-eyed child slid down from my lap and joined the others. I rendered a surprisingly full accompaniment. By the time Roz returned from the kitchen we were finishing up the first verse: *"And crown thy good with brotherhood from sea to shining sea!"*

My daughter and son were musical and sang in choirs all through their growing-up years. Even when Walter had stopped experimenting with Unitarianism, Ethical Culturism, Quakerism, mainstream Protestantism, they still sang in church choirs they chose themselves.

"Come with us," they'd say, and Walter and I would go hear the anthem, proud of our children's bright, trusting faces and strong voices. Walter was usually bored by the sermon, though sometimes, if the approach was what he called existential, by which I think he meant inquiring about life without a set of rules, he became quite interested. He did not like preconceptions. Walter was a devoted reader; he kept notebooks of quotations he liked. "Einstein developed his theory of relativity while working in the Swiss civil service," he said, his sweet, crooked smile coming and going. I called him my Einstein. He had no ambition to work outside of the Metropolitan Transportation Authority of New York City or to rise from his mid-management position in the accounting department. The children chose quotations from his notebooks—more than thirty spiral-bound notebooks over the years—to read aloud at his funeral. One sentence I remember, from Pascal: "Our whole dignity consists, then, in thought." That was my husband.

The weight of the blue-eyed child on my lap had calmed me.

Roz placed a white board on an easel in the front of the room and turned to the children. "What does it mean to say 'just as I am'?" She asked them to turn to the hymn that, with considerable improvisational skill, she'd adopted as the lesson of the morning. After several answers and a spirited discussion, it was decided that "just as I am" means being nobody except yourself.

"Do you have to be perfect for God to love you?" Roz asked.

"No!" came the antiphonal response.

"Do you have to wait until tomorrow to be yourself?"

"No!"

"Does God love you just as you are right now?"

"Yes!"

Roz asked every child to say his or her name, nobody else's. She wrote their names on the board. "Your very own name," she stressed. "And remember: God knows your name. He loves you just as you are today and just as you will be tomorrow."

Walter would have liked Roz's lesson. Start with the basics. Yourself. A few years after we'd been married, when I'd pretty much lined up with Walter and come to feel that I was up to any task I might encounter, we both still went to services to hear the kids sing. The four of us were near enough to see each other across the chancel, yet far enough to take our proper places with the collective choir and congregation. Sitting next to Walter, seeing the children in the choir, I was in balance. For me and, I think, for Walter, in those years God was "now-here."

There had been no room for a woman far away in a Missouri state penitentiary who might have ruined everything.

The children took their places at low tables and the room was filled with sounds of coloring, cutting, and pasting. A half hour later the last child left with her mother. Roz wrung out a sponge over a basin of soapy water.

"I like to talk to children about God," she said. She straightened one of the chairs and cocked her head. "You notice I don't say much about Jesus." She scooted another chair under the table. "Thank you for your help, Evelyn. You'd be a great addition to the literacy class, you know."

"It's been a wonderful hour," I admitted.

Raising her arms and soapy hands above her head, she yawned and performed several back and side stretches, more limber now that she wasn't covering herself with layers of clothing. She'd let the children and me see her wide, soft tummy, her single breast, her one shoulder higher than the other. The day before, she'd acknowledged that she would never camouflage herself with a special bra. "Just as I am," she'd said with a rueful smile.

Now she repeated, "You'd be superb help in the literacy class."

I scrubbed at a sticky spot on the table. "I don't want to teach in the prison."

Roz gave me a sharp glance, then turned away to hide her hurt feelings. "No? Okay."

"I'm just not up to it."

She gathered several paste jars together and supported them against her abdomen.

"It's the execution," I said. "Being across the street is

bad enough. I don't want to get any closer." I noticed the inconsistency; I wanted to see my mother, didn't I?

Roz carried the paste jars to the supply cabinet. "Do you have any relatives here? Anyone who's in touch with her?"

I knew of a great-aunt and uncle. I had no desire to see them.

Roz closed the cabinet. As she passed the piano, she lost her balance and dropped down hard onto the piano stool. Her face disintegrated and she cried out. "God!"

I dragged a child's chair across the floor and sat down beside her.

"Tim," Roz whispered, trembling.

I touched her hair. "How long have you known him?"

"Since he first got here." She counted on her fingertips. "Eight years." After an agonized silence she pushed against her knees and reared back violently. "We're such an immoral nation!"

"Certainly Tim Anguin is immoral," I said. It was unkind. *And so's your mother*, she could have shot back. But she merely stood and limped toward the children's coat hooks near the door. Chastened, I remained in the little blue chair.

Roz took her blouse and shawl from two of the hooks. Shrugging into her top layers, she spotted a stray rubber ball near the door and picked it up. "If you change your mind about the literacy class," she said, "let me know." Taking aim, she gave a practiced overhand toss. The ball landed in the toy box against the far wall. "Bingo," she said, turned on her heel, and slammed the door behind her.

I remained in the little chair a while before finally gathering my purse and umbrella. *Your daughter wants to see you, Mabel*, I imagined Roz saying to my mother. They would be on a first-name basis, *Mabel-ing and Roz-ing* each other with nonchalance.

I know, Roz, my mother would reply. *She comes during visiting hours and won't take no for an answer.*

What shall I tell her, Mabel?

Well, Roz, eventually she'll stop trying and then everything will be back to normal.

I feel kind of sorry for her, Mabel. Her husband just died. She's your daughter. She needs you. What shall I tell her?

Don't tell her anything, Roz. She'll get tired of trying. It took her forty years to get here. Leave her alone for a few weeks and she'll go back to New York...

Home again, I carried a folding chair from the card table to a window overlooking the back lawn. I could almost hear the afternoon breathing in and out. A vine once grew here, up the back of the house. In spring it curled its little green hands past the casement and onto the glass. Bees came to the window and buzzed around its purple flowers. My mother told me to sit very still and not be afraid of the buzzing. That way the bees would sense I was their friend.

As a child when I had trouble praying in church, I would look at the lavender tendrils curling within the stained-glass window and imagine the furry rumble, the motorized floating of bees just before they disappear, plump-rump-last, into the wisteria, and be able to pray.

Eight

Monday broke hot and humid. Everywhere there was a sizzle, like a neon tube going out. But until the light actually failed, protestors would mill about Capitol Avenue while the commercial interests on High Street would register the excited sputter of media and out-of-towners spending money in Jefferson City.

Coming out of my apartment early in the morning, I was already perspiring. Even in the rare moments when I didn't consciously think about the execution, the subject was always there, like a mild nausea. I had a brief image of myself crossing the street, floating through the limestone wall, waiting for Tim Anguin at the medieval-looking stone-and-dark-wood gas chamber pictured in the newspaper, its cross of pebbles embedded in the sidewalk. Descending my outside staircase, I performed moral long division on whether the Anderson babies drowned during a psychotic episode equaled a raped and murdered woman in Kansas City, and whether Tim Anguin or my mother was worse.

Though it was too early to drop in on Roz at eight in the morning, I turned down Cherry Street to be in her vicinity. Trixie of the black coat and white skull cap roused herself from where she'd been sleeping in front of the screen door, seated herself on the welcome mat, and began scrubbing her face with precise little circles. She paused, ambled down the porch steps, and crossed the lawn without curiosity. When she reached the sidewalk, she sidled up to the mailbox.

"Good morning, Trixie," I said, stooping to rub a plump jowl. She yawned elaborately, exposing a pink tongue and throat. Roz came out of the house wearing an ankle-length garment that was not quite a dress, not quite a bathrobe.

"I saw you out here," she said. "Come sit. I could use the

company."

I approached the porch. At the bottom step I looked up and saw that her crisp features had fallen into disrepair. Her mouth was loose and her eyes distracted. Only her nose was sharp. She gestured toward Trixie. I fell for the ruse and watched the cat lean like a drunk against the mailbox post, rubbing her ribs against the weathered wood. When I turned back, Roz was in the act of sitting down on the top step, crying.

"What is it?" I said.

"Can you go with me?"

I climbed the four steps and sat down beside her. "Where?"

She picked up her long skirt at the knee, bent her head, and wiped her eyes with the flowered fabric. "To the apartment building down the street from you."

I guessed she meant to Tim Anguin's girlfriend, the mystery woman in Steve's building.

"Tim is in very bad shape." She wadded and unwadded a Kleenex. "I wish I could change places with him. I'm getting old. I'm not well. The cancer could come back anytime. But he's a young man in his prime."

"Prime" didn't seem to be the right word. I tried to imagine what my husband might say to Roz. Pascal's dignity of thought would be inadequate to comfort her. My own storehouse of wisdom was empty. We sat for a while watching Trixie investigate the lawn, the geraniums, the top-heavy hollyhocks. Roz kicked off her pink flip-flops. When the sun broke above the roof of the house across the street, she stood. Dangling the sandals in one hand, she opened the screen door with the other and disappeared inside. She looked so ordinary that it seemed normal for there to be a prison two blocks away; normal for there to be an upcoming execution.

Trixie continued her exploration of grass and flowers. Next door an infant just learning to walk staggered onto his front porch in diapers, then squealed and tried to outrun his father who, close behind, scooped him up and roared like a bear into his tummy. I closed my eyes and lifted my face to the sun. I didn't see how Tim Anguin, having murdered the normal, the ordinary, deserved the wonderful commonplace of life.

Roz reappeared in a change of clothes and fresh makeup. We reached the corner and turned onto Capitol Avenue where the policemen in front of the prison kept their eyes on a space just above our heads, apparently a potential site of trouble. As we passed Glenn, Greenberry & Nixon, I glanced up at my curtainless windows. My apartment looked vacant, even to me.

"Tim gave me Sharon's address," Roz said. "He's never been there himself, of course."

"The ground-floor studio," I said.

She was surprised. "How do you know that?"

I was proud of my local knowledge. "Steve Mason told me." Two blocks away a demonstrator implored over a microphone, "Father, forgive them for they know not what they do."

"Why are we going to see her?" I asked.

"Tim wants me to tell her something."

"Why doesn't he tell her himself? During visiting hours."

"He can't bear her crying. He can't stand a scene now. He doesn't want to see her or talk to her anymore."

"Why have you brought me along?"

"No one else would come."

We trudged on. A police car rolled by, patrolling the length of the street. It made its U-turns in front of Glenn, Greenberry & Nixon. The crowd had grown large and noisy again. Singers were sounding more desperate and the hymns were rapid. Chanting verged on the hysteric. The old sociology professor with the veined legs and walking shorts still stood a little apart from the thick of things. Though his message, "'God bless us every one,' Tiny Tim," was oblique, I admired the signage with its single and double quotation marks. He could have been my scholarly husband twenty years in the future if the thinking had been more incisive and if Walter had been given twenty more years to live.

I felt my husband's hand at my back. When I remembered there was actually nothing touching me, that Walter would never touch me again, I stumbled. With a slightly fussy smile, the old gentleman reached out to steady me, but I moved on. The personality and height weren't Walter's, and Tiny Tim was no more steady than I.

We turned in at Steve's building and followed the walkway to the corner apartment. Roz knocked. Though we heard no footsteps, the door opened immediately, and the girl stood before us. She was wearing a short terry-cloth robe. Her single braid was gone, and she'd pulled her long hair back into a ponytail that swayed as she looked from Roz to me and back again. She looked younger than she had two nights earlier, but still, her hard gaze suggested experience. She would soon have lines.

"Tim asked me to see you. I'm Roz Teal and this is my friend Evelyn Grant Williams."

"I know who you are. Tim's told me."

Roz extended her hand. Sharon didn't take it. Roz was perspiring at the hair line. "May we come in for a moment?"

The girl's green eyes looked as if they'd been narrowing with suspicion since junior high. She reluctantly stepped back and we entered a single room with one window facing Capitol Avenue and the other facing east toward the warden's house. There was a fruity scent, not of fruit but of shampoo or hand lotion flavored with strawberry. Or maybe it was the gum she was chewing.

"I'd appreciate it if I could sit down," Roz said.

Aside from the pictures of Jesus on the corkboard above the table, the only decoration was a giant teddy bear fallen over on its side at one end of the sofa. Without permission, Roz took one of the two chairs at the narrow table. Used to being liked, she made a false start or two.

"Sharon," she finally said, "Tim asked me to come and talk

to you."

"Oh, yeah. You're the one who thinks she's his mother." The girl looked as fit and compact as a gymnast inside her beach cover-up. She folded her arms across her midsection. Her face, wider at the jaw than at the forehead, was fiercely guarded.

"Tim wants you to know he loves you very much."

"You don't have to tell me. I already know that."

"It's getting harder and harder for him now," Roz said.

"'Now'? It's been hard all along."

Roz put one hand up, palm-out. "Please!" she begged. She looked worse than she had on the porch step. With a quick movement she pulled her over-blouse across the flat side of her chest.

Sharon stamped her foot. "What are you doing here?"

"Tim doesn't want to see you today."

"You wish!" Sharon crouched and looked Roz in the eye. "I'll be at the prison at one o'clock. You can march right back to wherever you came from." It was an old-fashioned scolding. The words might have been her grandmother's.

Roz braced her weight against the table and struggled to stand. "Tim is in agony now."

"And I'm not?" Sharon yanked her short robe over her head and threw it at Roz before breaking into a wail. After a minute or two, she forced herself to be quiet. She was wearing a pink bikini. Her shoulders were shapely, her upper arms strong and well-defined. Without changing expression, Roz shook out the wadded-up terry cloth and conscientiously began turning it right-side-out. When she'd folded it neatly, she laid it across the back of the chair.

"The big mother!" Sharon shouted. She wriggled out of her bikini top, arched her back, and showed Roz her breasts. "Can you do *this*, Mother? Look! I've got two! Let's see yours!" She shot across the narrow space, breasts swaying, and grabbed the beach robe. Pulling it on as quickly as she'd yanked it off, she shouted, "Tell him what you saw! Tell him what I've got! Tell him—"

I opened the door and pushed Roz out ahead of me.

"He doesn't love you!" Sharon screamed behind us. The door slammed shut. I began crying from shock and because Sharon was young and alone. Because she was desperate for Tim. Because she was in competition with Roz and Roz was winning. Because there wasn't enough love to go around.

At the street Roz waited for me to catch up. "The girl is not right for Tim," she said, as if Tim had years to find the perfect woman. "She resents my closeness to him." She stumbled on a section of raised sidewalk. "Sharon thinks in sexual terms."

"Not much doubt about that," I said. And why wouldn't she? The bikini, designed for a swimming pool or beach, young people all around, had to serve in a studio apartment a half block from a prison. There was no one to admire her breasts.

"They've never slept together," Roz said. "They met through the United States Mail."

Had Sharon written to the condemned man, received a reply, and fallen in love with him long-distance? I constructed a quick fiction: Scene One. Roz institutes a letter-writing campaign on Tim's behalf. Scene Two. The Post Office delivers a rival.

The policeman made another U-turn in front of Glenn, Greenberry & Nixon. I stumbled on the same section of sidewalk that had just tripped Roz.

As the patrol car rolled westward down Capitol Avenue again, my mind strayed into another scene: the officer suddenly backs up with a squeal of rubber, runs up to the door, breaks it down, tries to arrest Sharon for lewdness inside her own home, is waylaid by desire, finds his way into her bikini, while the prisoners in the penitentiary at the end of the street begin flowing out of the front gates onto Capitol Avenue, following the helmeted police to Sharon's place.

Meanwhile, back in the prison, Tim sits on the edge of his cot with his head buried in his hands until Roz, advancing on death row at an ungainly trot, unlocks his cell, and, holding hands, they alternately run and limp (she from ill health, he from leg irons) the quarter of a mile to the Missouri River where a boat is tied up on shore from whence they head to St. Louis where, like Huck and Jim, they cross the Mississippi River into Illinois and Tim is free. With Roz forever.

Nine

A few minutes after one-o'clock visiting hours, Sharon came walking back from the prison. Sitting at my window, I watched her approach. Her hair, neither a ponytail nor a braid, hung limply, no line, no curl. If a twenty-year-old—actually, from a distance, she looked closer to sixteen—could be described as worn, Sharon was that twenty-year old. She moved sluggishly, nothing like the mermaid in the bikini this morning. Her jeans and top were shapeless. The angry face, hysteric green eyes, heightened color of this morning did not belong with the slumping body just reaching the property line of Glenn, Greenberry & Nixon. I hurried outside to the landing.

"Sharon?"

She looked up with a dazed expression. I came down the stairs and tried to join her on the sidewalk. Her forehead seemed narrower now than it had this morning, the jaw even wider. I was pretty sure Tim Anguin had refused to see her. Since she wasn't going to speak, I spoke first. "I feel terrible about this morning."

She kept on walking. I fell in behind her. "Are you going to work?"

No response.

I couldn't see her face, so I spoke to the sidewalk. "Keeping busy helps." We reached the corner of Capitol and Monroe. "If you have time, let's go up to Kelly's Café on High Street and have a bite to eat. My treat."

"I'm not hungry," Sharon said. Single-file, we turned up Monroe and covered a half block. Heat rose from the cement; words from the megaphone followed us.

"I'm hungry and I'd like company. I'm tired of eating alone."

Sharon stepped closer toward one edge of the sidewalk. I

moved up beside her, and wiped my forehead with a tissue.

"After my husband died I found I had to make myself eat." It wasn't an apt comparison. What nineteen- or twenty-year-old with a boyfriend on death row could care about middle-aged widowhood? We reached High. In front of Kelly's Cafe I touched Sharon's shoulder and lightly rotated her toward the entrance. She permitted the contact. At the back of the restaurant we slid into a booth.

"A Coke," Sharon said when the waitress came to the table.

I closed the soft, worn menu. "Two bowls of chicken soup."

"An order of toast," Sharon added. "Two eggs over easy." She started to shake out a cigarette but stopped and returned the pack to her cloth shoulder bag.

Often on days when Walter had eaten a large mid-day meal, he'd wanted only toast and butter for dinner, perhaps with a soft-boiled egg. I sometimes nagged him about cholesterol, but as it turns out, cholesterol doesn't matter when you're hit by a truck. I'd waited for him at the Algonquin Hotel where we were to meet for a drink and then go to the theatre. But he didn't come. I called our voice mail to see if he'd left a message. He hadn't, but the emergency room had.

The chicken soup arrived, and then Sharon's eggs.

"I have his motorcycle," the girl said, mechanically lifting the spoon to her mouth.

"What motorcycle?"

"Tim's."

I felt propelled toward a question that didn't interest me: "Where is it?"

Silence.

"Do you know how to ride a motorcycle?" I asked.

"Yeah. It's easy."

"I've never ridden one."

Sharon cleaned up her eggs in several fast bites. "How come you live across from the prison?" she asked, wiping her mouth.

"That's where I grew up."

"In a lawyer's office?"

"It was our family home back then."

She wrapped the second piece of toast in a napkin and put it in her bag.

"Have you seen Tim today?" I asked, sure of the answer.

She closed the bag and pinned me in a bold glance. "No, but Wednesday's a long way off."

"Right after Tuesday," I said. Hiking the strap of her bag over her shoulder, Sharon was ready to go. She hesitated long enough for me to add, "Sharon, you can come talk to me anytime you want to."

The girl swept the table, then me, with a glassy, exalted expression. Mentally, I withdrew.

In the process of hurrying from the Algonquin out onto the street, I'd lost my gloves. The taxi took me to Lenox Hill Hospital where I learned Walter had been struck by a vehicle at Lexington Avenue and 54th. I found him in the last cubicle to the left behind a sliding white curtain whose metal rings jingled on the steel track above him. I recognized him by his shoes. A young doctor pulled me away and led me into a small room painted bright yellow. She told me he'd died ten minutes earlier. It horrified me that my lovely, reasonable husband didn't know what had happened to him. A hospital chaplain came and accompanied me back to Walter. I threw myself onto his blood-soaked chest and tried to call him back. The chaplain held me by the shoulders and offered to pray, and I said Walter didn't want it. He asked me if I wanted to pray, and I said no. "Atheist," I said when I'd quieted enough to answer his question about religious preference. Before I left I was given a blue plastic bag with his bloody suit—hastily cut apart—and the latest issue of *Scientific American* he'd been reading. Someone from the hospital rode home with me in the cab and waited until I was inside my apartment building.

In bed that night, without his voice, his body, I understood that he'd been torn apart. Broken open. I understood that he was dead. With that knowledge, I broke, too. When the children arrived from California they had to hold me down. They nearly had to sit on me, they told me later.

As time passed, I stopped thinking about the accident. The manner of Walter's death became less compelling, less of an obsession, but it changed me. Alone, I crept through the weeks, grieving and frightened of dying, myself. Underneath the darkness that had opened over my head that night like the snap of a black umbrella, I tiptoed along, shielded from light and air.

But one day my rib cage, bored with shallow breathing, expanded and woke me with a stab of pleurisy. The pain was like a cry. I took down the umbrella and gulped air.

"I'm definitely going to Missouri," I told the children over the telephone.

By now they'd forgotten their advice about reconciliation and closure. There were long silences from both of them. "Why?"

"I can't go on feeling this bad. I have to do something."

"But Missouri isn't your home anymore, Mother. You live in New York. What about your job?"

They sounded like worried parents. In spite of their doubts and my own, I packed two bags. And now here I was, living in an empty apartment in Jefferson City, Missouri, watching a young woman suffer; thinking about a young man about to be executed; about a grieving, childless woman who voluntarily spent a large part of her life in prison; about a stubborn old woman, perhaps still insane, who wouldn't see her daughter.

I slid out of the booth and walked back down toward Capitol Avenue, the prison, the river, the railroad tracks. Those tracks ran east as well as west. All I needed was a ticket.

Seated in my apartment, Sharon leaned toward me conspiratorially. "He'll want to see me before Wednesday.

There's a lot of bullshit he has to go through right now." She even winked, as if no one could fool her about prisons and prisoners. She'd climbed the outside staircase a few hours after our lunch in Kelly's Café and looked at me with raw directness.

"Can I come in?"

I'd opened the screen door wider, surprised to see her.

"Of course." I pointed lamely to a folding chair. "I'm afraid I can't give you a comfortable place to sit." After looking around the room that must have seemed as empty and without interest as I, myself, Sharon said abruptly, "I'm going to tell you where his motorcycle is because there's nobody else I can tell."

But she delayed the confidence and began uttering platitudes in pearly tones that echoed in the high-ceilinged room. She liked her waitress job at the hotel, she said, where "they treat me right." She liked Jefferson City. She liked shopping for clothes at the mall. She liked her apartment. She liked a big town. There seemed to be a hundred things she liked. Nothing about a gas chamber. Finally she stopped talking. Her complexion turned blotchy and her green eyes glittered with futile excitement.

"A couple of months ago Tim gave me an address in Kansas City. He told me to pick up his Harley and ride it to my mom and dad's." She waited, as if I might prod her into telling where her parents lived, where she'd grown up, why at her age she wasn't living at home, why she wasn't in school, how she'd gotten mixed up with Tim in the first place.

She moved her folding chair closer. "I left Kansas City after dark. I didn't stop until I got to the Ozarks. The trees were about to leaf out. I could see the buds, little bumps along the branches, in the moonlight. It was just the motorcycle and me, but I felt like Tim was with us."

The street lamps on Capitol Avenue came on early, squandering their light.

"But my dad found it two weeks later behind his welding shop. I hid it under a tarp but you can't fool my dad. He told me

I couldn't keep it there, so I rode it to Jefferson City."

"Sharon," I said, "who's going to be with you day after tomorrow?"

The girl stared into empty space for a moment. That was when she grinned like a conspirator. Leaning forward, amused, as if I were a dear, silly thing for worrying, she confided—no, promised—Tim would see her before Wednesday, as if time were slowing for the two of them; as if Wednesday weren't two actual days into the future; as if Tuesday and Thursday didn't lie on either side of a real day.

"*He'll* be with me. He has a plan. He'll see me before Wednesday and tell me everything I need to know."

"What makes you so sure?"

Her bravado faded. Clearly, I didn't understand. Flat, green-glass surface replaced the glitter in her eyes. Her thickened lids hung low. The kettle in the kitchen whistled. When I returned, she hadn't moved. Steam and the scent of jasmine uncoiled from the cups and rose toward the light fixture in the ceiling.

"I guess you don't care where the motorcycle is." She fiddled with her blouse. She put her hands together and brought them up—large hands I'd failed to notice before, with rough cuticles and knuckles—until the fingertips touched her chin. "It's in the woods behind my apartment."

I didn't pretend to care, but she continued. "I think Tim wants me to move it."

"He could see you during visiting hours and tell you what he wants done with it," I said. "That way, you wouldn't have to guess."

She ignored the remark. "Can you help me?" She braced against the edge of the metal chair and, with her feet just off the floor, lifted herself an inch or two before letting herself down again. She was the kind of girl who can chin herself and do push-ups.

"You do realize, don't you, Sharon, that day after tomorrow he's going to die?" After Walter's death someone had told me that reality is the safest place. I'd resented the comment. Sharon continued to raise and lower herself off the chair seat. It tipped and her mask cracked. "Shit!"

Coaxing her to her feet, I led her, sobbing, not to a sofa, because there wasn't one, but to the air mattress in the bedroom. I sat her down, wedged a pillow between her back and the wall, then knelt at the foot. Faint light from the living room reached us.

"You know, Sharon, I have someone across the street, too."

She was not interested.

"It's my mother. And she doesn't want to see me, either."

"He'll see me, he'll see me," she whispered, and was seized by violent hiccups.

I made simple, trite observations about getting through a bad time. Whether she was paying attention, I didn't know. Eventually she closed her eyes and fell asleep.

After moving the two folding chairs back to their original positions and washing the teacups, I sat down in the living room. From two blocks away a few tireless demonstrators continued their hymn-singing. When I found myself nodding off, leaning precariously to one side of the folding chair, I went into the bedroom. Fully dressed, I lay down on one side of the air mattress, careful not to wake Sharon, and stared into the darkness until I, too, fell asleep.

The chatter of birds woke me at dawn. The air was pleasantly cool. I moved quietly about the rooms, washing up, changing into fresh clothes, making coffee. I cooked two bowls of oatmeal and carried them to the card table. But when I went in to wake Sharon, the room was empty. She'd smoothed the pillow and sheets and left a note on the bed: "Gone to work."

Having approximated motherhood for a few hours, I could not bear to be alone. No exercise of memory could soothe the ache along the insides of my arms and wrists. I missed my children and husband. As I roamed about the apartment, my mind admitted anything and everything flitting by: Sharon outside the prison wall calling to Tim Anguin. Her father ripping the tarp off Tim's motorcycle with a single swipe of his beefy hand. Steve's dubious expression when I talked about the Grant family's good behavior. Roz's Oxfords hooked around the rung of the folding chair.

I found myself mentally crossing the alley, creeping into our back neighbors' house, up the stairs into the nursery, over to the crib; watching my mother put a baby under each arm, cross the hall, lay them gently in the bathtub. I think she laid a stopper, yellowed rubber, cracked, over the drain. She would have turned on the water faucets. I even imagined the detail of water temperature. It was mixed, not too hot, not too cold. At least the children weren't scalded. It made her seem better. The rounded edge of the high tub, the kind that has feet and stands off the linoleum floor, bruised my ribs as I leaned into it. The infants' mouths were open, but there was no sound.

Ten

Roz's old Lincoln disappeared, then reappeared from the opposite direction. She'd overshot my apartment. Stopping abruptly in the middle of the street, she went through her incompetent parking routine, backward, forward, closer to the curb, farther from the curb, until, piece-by-piece, she finally emerged from the driver's side: thick ankle, long chiffon skirt, plump hand with bright pink fingernails, paisley blouse, paisley over-blouse, velvet quilted shoulder bag, long silk scarf, and, at the top, straw hat with flowers surrounding the crown. She managed to slam the car door shut without catching herself or her garments, and labored up the sidewalk.

I opened the door while she was still climbing the staircase. "They let you past the barricades?"

"It's all right," Roz panted, "as long as I get my car off the street by eight." Bright sunlight dazzled the east side of the house. One block west, the demonstrators were resuming their hymn pretty much where they'd left off the night before.

I squinted at my watch. "It's nearly eight now."

She came in, sat down heavily on a metal chair, and smoothed her skirt across her stolid knees spread slightly in a we-don't-try-to-look-shapely position.

"You're out early this morning."

"I couldn't sleep," she said. "I felt like dropping in." Being dropped in on—first by Sharon, now Roz—made me almost a Missourian again. No one in New York just drops in. In fact, New Yorkers rarely enter each others' apartments. They meet for lunch or coffee or drinks.

"Are you going to the special service for Tim?" Roz asked.

"At the Methodist Church? I don't think so. I've been sleeping poorly. I guess you're on your way there?"

Roz began flapping the large scarf draped around her neck. "I'm sick of church. I can't bear to hear another prayer for Tim." She stopped fanning herself, an exertion that could only have made her warmer, and flung a plump arm and paisley sleeve in the direction of the demonstrators on Capitol Avenue. "They don't know Tim. For them, he's just an excuse to be for or against the death penalty."

"Have you eaten breakfast?"

"I'm not hungry." Roz glared at the blank walls. "No offense, Evelyn, but when are you going to stop camping out?"

"I told you. I'm here temporarily." Suddenly I did not want her black Oxfords planted on my floor or those stolid legs jeopardizing my folding chair.

Roz shifted on the metal seat. "I'm not hungry but I could use a cup of tea."

"No tea," I said. "The campfire died. Besides, there isn't time. You have to move your car."

Roz shot a sharp glance from under the straw brim. "Did Sharon visit you yesterday?"

"I don't remember inviting you to my campout," I retorted. "Have you been spying on me?"

"My neighbor was driving by and saw Sharon come out of your apartment early this morning."

"Sharon is lonely and terrified," I said. "She came to talk and ended up sleeping over. I'm very sorry for her."

"Sorrier than you are for Tim."

Bless Tim Anguin, I thought in a knee-jerk prayer for prisoners before adding, "But he's a rapist and murderer."

Roz stood and moved surprisingly fast toward the door. "The state penitentiary is across the street, Evelyn. We're always going to have criminals in Jefferson City. If you wait for everyone in this town to be good, you'll have a long wait." She passed one hand over her forehead. The hat slipped sideways. "We're always going to have the wall. But limestone is soft." She righted the hat. "People change."

I did not want a lecture on crime and how criminals change. I had not seen change in my mother. I had not seen my mother at all. Feeling both ostentatious and melancholy, I shooed Roz out onto the landing. Down at the curb, a breeze blew her scarf and long skirt eastward. She stumbled and nearly fell. I hurried down.

"That was close," she said, leaning against the car, panting.

I waited until I was sure she could stand alone.

"Can't you take a ride with me?" she begged. "Just to get away."

I glanced down Capitol Avenue. I was standing at the center of a fresh, sunny day from fourth grade when birds sing and you're walking to school with a friend. Your wonderful teacher, Miss Schroer or Miss Beek or Miss Benninghoff, is waiting for you. You hear the bright, slightly desperate chirps and squeals of your classmates who are flinging themselves about the playground in a futile effort to forget that the janitor, old Mr Brockman, is slowly climbing from the furnace room to stand at the front entrance and ring the brass bell. And then you remember today is music day, or art day, or your Brownies' meeting day, and that after school your mother will be in the lunch room because that's the Brownies' meeting room, and she, along with Mrs Nixon, is one of the troop leaders, and you're ecstatic and you break into a run.

The fourth grade is over in the blink of an eye, and you never forget it.

I got into the car. I didn't care that I was about to spend the morning with Roz, or that I'd left the door to my apartment wide open.

The car lurched forward. Somewhere in the neighborhood an old manual lawnmower was busy, the kind I'd grown up hearing on hot Missouri mornings. I remembered precisely the sound of whirring blades, tinny thrashing, the herbal smell of a lawn whose patches of high grass diminish, turn by turn. If you get too near the mower, flying grass sticks to your hot, moist legs. You itch all day until, late in the afternoon, you're called in for a cool bath and change of clothes. Dinner is on the screened-in porch. Later, in darkness, you and your friends catch fireflies in mayonnaise jars, conscientiously punching holes in the waxed-paper-and-rubber-band tops. But there's never enough air, and the next morning the fireflies at the bottom of the jar are tough little bits of debris rattling against the glass.

At the corner, Roz waved to one of the helmeted officers standing at the prison entrance. "That's Roger. I taught his son in Sunday School, then again behind the walls."

"I guess Sunday School didn't have much effect."

Without taking her eyes off the road, she shook a tissue out of her purse. "Nothing I've done has had much effect." She dabbed at her forehead and upper lip. "I've made so many mistakes."

I didn't want to hear the list.

At a red light she jammed her foot on the brake. "You haven't made any?"

"Mistakes?"

"That's what we're talking about."

"No, that's what *you're* talking about."

The light turned green. "You romanticize the past, Evelyn. That's your mistake."

"*You* romanticize Tim Anguin."

"He's a wonderful person, Evelyn. His life is tragic and his death will be tragic." Her face disintegrated. "He needs me. He needs a friend. I would do anything to help him live."

We drove a block in silence before she pulled her face together, sharp nose, smart eyes, bow mouth—"Sharon!"—and sniffed with contempt.

"Since we're speaking of Sharon—"

"No, *you're* speaking of Sharon."

"—does Tim not want to see Sharon? Or do *you* not want him to see her?"

She removed her straw hat and threw it into the back seat.

"That doesn't deserve a response."

We drove along a road that passed mixed-use parcels: houses with chickens in the yard. Two boarded-up filling stations. Parallel to and above what I still thought of as the new highway cutting through town, Roz turned left onto an overpass. Blasted-apart limestone cliffs, pulverized fossils, rose straight up on either side of the sunken roadway below. I imagined myself swinging from the bluff, legs pedaling air, while below, two small figures, Roz and Sharon, spiral down toward the cars racing north and south. And isn't that Tim Anguin twirling by? I've never seen him but I know immediately who he is. Such good looks for such a bad man. Face and bone structure as clean and neat as a good conscience. Roz reaches out to catch his hand. Sharon reaches, too, but he drifts by both of them. Always drifting past women, mothers and lovers, unless he's savaging them. Always leaving them empty-handed, jealously eyeing each other.

We'd crossed over to the South Side, "German Town" as it was still called when I was a girl. Nineteenth-century houses with arched windows, decorative brackets, round tower rooms glided by, stable, sane, beautiful. Roz stopped abruptly and pulled over to the curb in front of an abandoned Victorian set back from the street, its doors and windows broken out. I studied the only derelict house on the block. Once again Roz had gravitated to the dysfunctional. She sat chewing on a cuticle.

"I need help. I can't get through this Tim Anguin business alone. In another month I can handle the teaching myself, but just now... "

"Why have we come to German Town?"

"It's not German Town."

"It used to be."

"It's the South Side now, Evelyn."

"What are we doing here?"

"Killing time until Ted Baldwin's shift begins."

"We could have killed time somewhere else. And who's Ted Baldwin: another one of your protégés?" I opened the door. I could walk home from here.

"A guard I know well. He'll let us through the gate." Roz spoke faster. "Please come to the prison with me for an hour or so. I can do some organizing in the classroom. I can't bear to be out here while Tim is behind the wall." She gripped my arm. "He feels like my child. The prison feels like home." She turned away. "I don't have children of my own."

"They won't let me through the gate."

"They'll let you through," Roz assured me. "I told them you're my assistant teacher. Ted will escort us in right behind the pastor."

"They won't let me in," I repeated. "There's an execution next week."

"The prison is almost empty now." She gave a toss of her head. "Except for Tim, security is light. It's mostly the old inmates left behind."

"What about all the police out front?"

"Show of force," said Roz. She turned the key in the ignition. "Ted Baldwin and the other guards trust me. And between you and me, *they* run the prison, not the administrators or the Governor."

I was letting Roz take me inside the walls. I'd wanted to do it myself.

"Pull out your driver's license," she instructed back at the house. We hurried inside just long enough to leave our purses and Roz's hat on her dining room table before we began walking up Cherry Street toward the prison. At first she seemed slow. I found myself wanting to run ahead, touch the wall before she got there. But when I thought about actually seeing my mother—would I recognize her? would she recognize me? would she turn her back? open her arms?—I fell behind.

Keeping her eyes on the entrance one block ahead, Roz held to a steady pace until a black, four-door car crossed the intersection and came to a stop in front of the police lined up at the gate.

"Move," she said, and began a modified speed-walk. "I want us to be there when the minister steps out of the car."

"Doesn't he have an office in the prison?"

"This isn't the prison chaplain," Roz panted.

When we got closer I recognized the Methodist minister. Roz's timing was perfect. The pseudo-trot ended precisely in front of Reverend Schmidtke at the exact moment he stepped out of the back door. She even managed to be at the right distance to shake his hand. "Good morning, Pastor." He greeted both of us gravely by name, lending me a legitimacy I didn't feel.

Our little group—Roz, Reverend Schmidtke, three guards, and I—watched the black car turn around and disappear up Cherry Street. Behind the row of State police, the double-gated stone entrance waited to swallow us into the body of the penitentiary. Bless the inmates, I prayed mechanically. Then, bless my mother. A knot of fear, excitement, forbidden interest began to form in the pit of my stomach. Forbidden because, at the same moment I held back, I wanted to rush through the gate, blunder headlong into the prison, and hunt her down. *Mother! How could you not want to see me!* Hug her. Hug the life out of her. Although the prison wall existed to protect people outside from the people inside, in rare cases it could be the other way around. The knot in my stomach became a cramp. I needed a bathroom.

"Stay right with us," said one of the guards. I followed the entourage into the prison. A young officer, isolated in a metal cubicle just inside the entrance, looked twice at my out-of-state license. Surely I would be stopped and ejected. I wanted to be stopped and ejected. He glanced at Roz who cocked her head knowledgeably. He checked his computer screen, stamped my hand with purple ink, and waved me to the next station.

The first and second metal doors clanged shut behind us. When the echoes finally stopped, gates opening ahead of us took up the sound. I, like my mother, would no more be allowed to leave these spaces than the gates that, hurling themselves open and shut, could stop their sound bouncing off the bilious green walls. At the end of each corridor I turned to see if an old woman was following us.

We reached an elevator the size of a box car. Reverend Schmidtke stepped in, a guard on either side. Roz and I were let off first. Preceding us down a hallway that branched off yet again, Ted Baldwin, a bow-legged man, not as tall and beefy as a guard ought to be, unlocked the door to the classroom, and—left us alone. I was anxious for Roz to snap on the lights. Under the humming fluorescents, I scanned the corners. Though she wasn't visible, my mother seemed present. Certainly she was near.

"I guess this room is searched before and after every class," I said.

"Yes, I often find things rearranged." Severe, highly motivated, Roz removed her scarf and began pulling drawers from the large desk at the front of the room. After emptying them, she turned each one upside-down over the wastebasket, gave a thump to its plywood bottom, then blew clouds of dust and gray fluff from the corners before returning it to its sliders and slots. "They rearrange but never clean," she said.

Of all the places Roz could have gone today, a multitude of Jefferson City clubs and organizations of which she was a member, she was here in the prison doing something I doubted she did much at home: cleaning. This is where her life had brought her: to the state penitentiary. I couldn't help noticing the same thing about myself. Roz shook her chestnut curls. Since chemotherapy treatments, her hair had grown in thick and glossy.

"I'd rather be here than home," she said. "I never like going home, even in the best of times. Being out, away, gives me relief from my shortcomings."

If anything was designed to remind one of one's shortcomings, it was a prison. I didn't want to be pulled into Roz's regrets again. I crossed to a window and looked out through the bars at a green expanse of lawn scarred by sidewalks. Looming off to the left was a building as large as a hangar. Several stories high, it was riddled with narrow, barred windows. With its gloomy face and limestone opening, it appeared to have crawled up from the prison quarry a century ago.

I stared until my eyes watered. At this very moment my mother might be looking out from one of those windows. My heart almost ripped apart: I wanted to be seen. *Over here, Mother!* I heard myself give out one sob, and coughed to disguise the sound.

"I should have left Jefferson City," Roz was saying. "I haven't lived my life the way I planned. So much has gone wrong."

I remained looking out the window.

"I'm ashamed." Roz tucked her head into her neck. "I'm ashamed of my weight and just having one breast and a shaved head and being clumsy and—"

I mouthed a compliment. "Your hair is beautiful now."

"—and losing my husband to another woman—"

I moved away from the window.

"—and losing my baby."

In the front row I seated myself in a student desk. I hadn't known about her baby.

"People think I'm—well, whatever they think I am. But I'm not. Not at all." In town, the Courthouse clock began to strike twelve noon. At a distance I could see the mansard roof of my parents' house riding above the wall.

In the cement corridor outside, footsteps sounded. Roz blew her nose. The door opened and a tall black man wearing round, wire-rimmed spectacles entered the room. He could have been sixty. He could have been eighty. He came over to the desk and clasped Roz's hand, not in a handshake or high-five, but an intimate finger weave between friends.

"Little lady," he said sorrowfully, studying her crumpled face. She squeezed his hand and swung it in a fond arc.

"The river is deep," he said.

Roz broke down into her handkerchief. Re-emerging, she gestured toward me and spoke thickly: "Ezekiel, I want you to meet Evelyn Grant Williams. She's going to help us with the class." Before I could demur, Roz added, as if closing a sale, "I brought her by to meet you and hear you read."

I wondered why, if he was a prisoner, he was walking around by himself. Grudgingly, I admired her for being able to grieve for Tim and pursue her search for a teaching assistant at the same time. But I was embarrassed for Ezekiel, as if he were trained to perform on demand. Apparently accustomed to her recruiting efforts, he reached across Roz's desk in one smooth motion and picked up a book. Cradled in his hand, it looked small. He came over to the front row of desks, sat down beside me, and opened to a pink, dog-eared bookmark sticking out of Ernest Gaines's *A Lesson Before Dying*.

Thrusting his head back a few inches in order to see out of his bifocals, he began: "Jefferson was asleep or pretended to be asleep when they got to the cell." His voice was deep, with a Missouri or even farther-south accent. He guided himself through the sentences with a blunt-nailed forefinger. If he didn't know a word, he paused, taught it to himself, and continued. He read about a prison in the Deep South many years earlier. There was a character named Jefferson, and a big, rural woman who loved him like her child; there was a skeptical, uncomfortable narrator. Ezekiel read with gravity. Ezekiel *was* gravity. This man with a face of dark, glowing planes was bringing me down to earth, away from mood swings and extremes. He was bringing Roz down, too. We listened, calmed. At the end of the chapter he closed the book over his index finger.

Who is Jefferson? Who is Miss Emma? I wondered.

Without wasting time, yet in no hurry, Ezekiel unfolded himself from the desk. "I've got to be going. I just stopped by to say hello." On his way out he looked back at me. "You say 'Grant' was your name?"

I nodded.

"There was a Dr Grant who used to come by the hospital ward years ago."

"That was my father." My palms cooled at the same moment they broke out in perspiration. I was proud; I was ashamed.

"What happened to him?" Ezekiel asked.

"He died a long time ago." One day my grandparents in Idaho received a letter from Mexico City that he was dead. They didn't talk about him and neither did I.

"He had a good reputation among us."

"Have you been here—a long time?" I asked. "Did you know him?"

"I've been here most of my life. I knew *of* him."

The memory of my father's face, voice, zigzagged through me as Ezekiel left the room. Roz pulled out paperwork. Picking up a dust cloth from a stack she'd brought with her, I walked to the bookshelf in the back of the classroom.

"Where is the hospital ward?" I asked when we'd been working for several minutes.

"In one of the newer buildings."

"Where was it in the '40s and '50s?"

"I think on the top floor of the building we're in now."

I started toward the windows, then stopped. These windows couldn't be opened. Here, I couldn't do something as simple as shake a dust cloth out a window.

"Put it in this and take a clean one," Roz said, handing me a plastic bag. "I wash them at the laundromat."

"I'll wash them in the lawyers' washer and dryer," I said.

Roz turned back to her work.

"My parents' old Maytag was in the basement," I added.

"Uh-huh."

"Then my father bought my mother an automatic machine."

"I'll be finished with this report in a minute, Evelyn."

"Do they just let prisoners wander around by themselves?" I asked after a few minutes.

"Not usually. He's a trusty. Unpaid staff, you might say."

"Why don't they just let him go free? He's old. He's paid his debt."

"He's old but not free, Evelyn. There are rules and regulations."

"What a tragedy," I said. "Such a wonderful man spending his life here." I hesitated. "What did he do?"

Roz capped her pen and closed the file in front of her. "Oh, I think murder, when he was young." Crime no longer appalled her.

Stepping to the window again, I imagined my father and Ezekiel walking between rows of hospital beds in the ward upstairs. I'm there, too. I'm my parents' child again. My father is buoyant; I remember he smiled often, rising on the balls of his feet to make a point. Beside him, a young Ezekiel carries out my father's instructions for relieving pain and saving lives. By slipping shining white enamel over Ezekiel's bad teeth, filling in the bald nest on the crown of his head, returning his wiry white hair to black, I can make him young again. I don't have to smooth his skin; it is still smooth.

And there I am. Ezekiel and I are working in the ward along with my parents. They're teaching us to operate the X-ray machine. All four of us will take turns operating the machine. We'll share heroic duties, such as pounding on patients' stopped hearts and setting in motion Code Blues, as well as humbler tasks: giving baths and emptying bed pans. With Dr Grant at the head of the team, we run a very good hospital ward. We're doing useful work together. It really doesn't matter that we're in prison.

My father doesn't pray; he employs scientific methods. And he is a living example of self-control. My parents are an unbeatable duo: one prays while the other lives by facts. My parents are fond of Ezekiel, this handsome young man with good teeth and a full head of hair. They think he would be a good son-in-law. They encourage us to fall in love. When we do, they approve. Ezekiel and I will carry on the family. Race is no impediment to anything. The engagement announcement, engagement party, wedding shower, rehearsal dinner, the ceremony itself, will all take place in the Missouri State Penitentiary. My parents are proud. The wedding is acknowledged by all, reported in the News and Tribune, attended by family and friends who think a prison setting is unique. Picturesque. The parents of the murdered babies are invited; they've forgiven my mother for her crime against them because she was temporarily insane, and anyway, maybe the babies aren't really dead after all. We've become a very special family, held in the arms of the State of Missouri. The marriage is auspicious.

But when it's time for the two of us to leave the ward and make our own way in life, we are stopped. Ezekiel committed a capital offense, after all, and must stay in prison. Alone, I go out in the world where I am fortunate enough to find Walter. When I bring him back to the ward to meet my parents, they like him immediately. I introduce him to Ezekiel and the two men become fast friends.

Responding to Walter's polite but persuasive request for Ezekiel's release, the State of Missouri grants him freedom. We three youths wave good-bye to Dr and Mrs Grant standing by the X-ray machine smiling. We pass through the prison gates where we proceed to the Capitol grounds and frolic across green expanses of lawn. There's no such thing as prison and death. No such thing as rape and murder and drowned babies. Walter will never die. I will never suffer. And no one is stopping us, two whites and a Negro, from having fun together. There's no such thing as race or sex. There may be a hint here and there that Walter and Ezekiel and I have bodies. Just possibly the young men's bodies make me want to stretch; flaunt myself. But that's nice. The sexual stirrings in my body are nice, and in the men's bodies, too. These nice stirrings lead to nothing. Nothing in the 1950s and 1960s is complicated or difficult except in China and Japan and Korea and Eastern Europe, Viet Nam, Birmingham, Selma, Kent State, but that will all change because the United States will make things nice all over the world...

I look up. I haven't been hallucinating like my mother; merely digressing.

Footsteps echoed somewhere down a corridor. In the distance, gates opened and closed; my bowels churned. I'd almost forgotten where I was or that I needed a bathroom.

"I have to go home," I said to Roz.

She closed up her desk, gathered a few papers, and got to her feet, as reluctant to leave as I was to stay.

"I've had enough of the past," I stated firmly. I didn't like being near what used to be the hospital ward. I didn't like knowing it was somewhere above me in this very building. The top floor where my father had consulted bore down on me with the weight of personal history. The hospital ward gave me foolish fantasies. Faulty thinking. Here in the prison where my parents' lives had been ruined, I had been pretending to be a child. I was regressing in Jefferson City, letting Roz draw me closer and closer to my mother, like a moth to a flame, whereas I had wanted to approach her in my own way, craving warmth while trying not to be burned.

Roz looked at me sideways. "I thought the past is why you're here."

"You'll see that I'm very much a woman of the present."

"And a very fine woman she is, she is, she is." Roz closed the door behind her and entered the corridor with a rhythmic sway, a nursery rhyme chant, a Gilbert and Sullivan-like ditty she found amusing. But I found *Roz* amusing; no, ridiculous. I would leave her far behind, limping in her overweight, off-balance, one-breasted, one-woman parade behind these walls.

I didn't need anything from her or from her prison. I'd leave them all behind: my mother, my father, Roz, Sharon, Tim, Ezekiel, everyone and everything.

Once outside the walls, I'd stay outside the walls. I'd join clubs. I'd go to church. I'd take rides with Steve. I'd be normal again. I'd walk about town, not because I was trying to kill time, but because I wanted to see, really see, the lawns and stately sculptures of the Capitol grounds; the South Side with its fine German homes; the hilly East Side with its red brick Lincoln University. The world called me with its color and movement. And then in August or September I would return to New York, a complete woman who had erased her grief. I did not need to see my mother after all.

Eleven

Tuesday afternoon, half way through another damp, disgruntled nap on the air mattress, I was awakened by a sudden blast from the megaphone: "Just as I am!" The afternoon oozed and glistened like one of the tar patches on the pavement in front of the prison. By the time I set out for the library with a blue umbrella in one hand and a book bag over my shoulder, the light was changing. Thunderheads traveled toward Capitol Avenue from the west. The faithful elderly professor, steaming under a transparent raincoat through which his walking shorts and varicose veins were visible, stood on the corner gripping his "Tiny Tim" sign. Covered with plastic sheeting today, the hand lettering rippled and fluttered wherever a damp gust of wind found an opening.

A figure a half block ahead turned in at the side door of the Methodist Church and disappeared. As I approached the same spot I realized the ponytail, cutoffs, and halter top did not add up to just any figure. It was Sharon. I turned the corner and hesitated at the front entrance of the church. A flash of lightning overhead triggered rain. I climbed the water-specked steps to the sanctuary, and in the dim light of the empty church, slid into my mother's pew. On a dark afternoon, stained-glass windows cast no bright colors or glowing patterns across empty benches and a cold altar. I sat quietly, mechanically going through a few short Tim Anguin prayers the way an absent-minded Catholic might finger a rosary.

When my eyes had adjusted to the light, I saw Sharon seated close to the chancel rail. I forgot about praying. I slid out of my mother's pew, and, with one hand on the finial beside the girl, indicated the wish to sit beside her. Stone-faced, she slid over and made room. I hooked my umbrella on the hymnbook rack. Rain drummed on the roof. Sitting away from my mother's pew removed the compulsion to pray.

I panned from the nearest stained-glass window down to the minister's tall chair with its wooden headrest carved in intricate thorns and crowns, and closer, to the starched white altar cloth directly in front of me. Again my gaze drifted upward, this time to the choir loft where my father had sung bass in the back row. As a soloist he'd often brushed by the tenors, altos, and sopranos until he stood alone beside the pipe organ, brilliant in his maroon choir robe, not a large man but a confident man who had mastered "The Refiner's Fire" from the *Messiah*. His rich voice carried the long line of many notes in one breath: "re-fi-i-i-i-i-i-i-ner's fi-i-ire."

"What do you want?" Sharon said.

The coffin for Tim Anguin would have already been built. He was so close to being a corpse that the technical death tomorrow was almost unnecessary. A reflex prayer kicked in again. *Tim will be redeemed by Christ's love.* But the desultory meditation was cold ashes compared to my father's fi-i-ire.

"I just want to sit here," I said. This hard-faced girl with her low-class manners and desperate motorcycle stories might, at this very moment, be redeeming Tim, propelling him by prayer to—wherever people go in order to be changed. Limestone walls crumble, Roz had said. People change. I tried again. Christ. The cross. Fi-i-ire.

She stood. "I'm leaving."

I twisted sideways so she could get by. "Have you been praying?" I asked, looking up at her.

"Why else would I be here?"

"I wish I could pray," I confessed. "That's one reason I came down to sit by you. You seem to know what you're doing." I followed her up the aisle. Passing through the double doors of the sanctuary and descending the short flight of stairs to the wet street, we turned left toward High as if we were going to town together. I put up the umbrella, a blue dome under which we walked in tinted light.

"Are you working today?" It would be the late shift at the hotel if she was.

"I quit my job."

Rain beat on the umbrella. Sharp drops of warm rainwater drove into my elbows and feet, anything that extended beyond the blue waterproofing.

"What do you want?" she asked me again.

"I don't know," I said. "I guess to be near you."

"Why?"

"We both have someone in prison."

She didn't respond.

"Were you praying for Tim?" I asked.

"Of course. Weren't you praying for your mother?" She got out from under the umbrella and walked ahead of me.

I walked faster. "I don't really know how to pray anymore," I said.

She tossed her head, as if to say *I can't teach you*.

I caught up to her and we walked side by side under the umbrella again. "What will you do after Wednesday?" I asked.

She ignored me.

"Will you go back home? Do you have plans?"

She stopped abruptly. "Plans?" We were in front of the Courthouse. I lifted the umbrella higher. The wind blew short hairs, the ones not caught up in her ponytail, about her face. Half inside, half outside the blue light, she gave me a sudden, pointed look. "Yes, I have plans." Red threads lay tangled in the whites of her eyes. Her wide jaw was knotted. "You're a friend of Roz."

I nodded. Sort of a friend. Kind of a friend. But I didn't quibble.

"Will you ask her if you can take her place visiting Tim this afternoon?"

"They won't let me—"

She rushed on. "I want you to tell him something private for me."

"Even if I were allowed in, Sharon, which I won't be, the guards will be listening."

She ignored me. "It's a code we worked out. He'll understand." Color climbed her face, and she grew almost breathless as she careened into her message: "'Mary' is motorcycle.' 'Church' is where I'm living. So if you say Mary is waiting behind the church, he'll know the motorcycle is behind my apartment house."

I was astonished that she believed this silly code would help a man on death row. "Sharon, how would he possibly get to the motorcycle? He's heavily guarded."

Lightning snapped and arced just a street or two over, it seemed. Jefferson City was a match with a bright blue head and God was striking it against his thumbnail. I was afraid for Tim: Tomorrow he was going to Hell.

Sharon grasped my arm. "Please see him."

"You would have to do that, yourself, Sharon."

The dark circles under her eyes almost had a voice. She shrugged hopelessly. A sudden blast of wind and rain nearly tore the umbrella out of my hands. I tilted into the storm. Each time I took a step, Sharon tugged at my elbow.

"Where did this idea about the motorcycle come from?" I almost shouted.

"From Jesus!"

I stopped. "You have to be careful about what you think Jesus is telling you." Rain bounced even harder off the hot sidewalk, biting into our feet and ankles, soaking our sandals.

Sharon stopped, too. "Take this with you when you go," and she opened her water-logged cloth bag, tipping it so I could see the gun inside.

"I'm not going anywhere, Sharon," I snapped, holding the umbrella at arm's length where it gusted this way and that, out of control. "You're carrying a weapon. Right in front of the

Courthouse, too. Do you want to end up in prison, yourself?" She stared and backed away from what must have seemed a mild-mannered woman, me, gone berserk. Her idiocy infuriated me. I regained control of the umbrella and began a quick trot toward High Street.

"Wednesday is tomorrow!" Sharon shouted, following me through the rain. "Something has to be done before tomorrow!"

Facing into the wind, I shouted back, "There are metal detectors! Security! They search everyone!"

Sharon caught up. "This gun is different."

I couldn't imagine what she was talking about. I started across High against a red light. Sharon grabbed me and pulled me back to the gutter.

"What do you mean, 'this gun is different'?" I stormed.

She dropped my arm and laughed. "It's invisible!" Her face was as changeable as an eel. I thought she'd gone insane. "You don't even know when someone's joking!" She wheeled in the opposite direction and yelled over her shoulder, "You're pathetic! Your mother doesn't want to see you!"

I stood at the curb and watched her figure diminish as she ran down the Monroe Street hill. I followed, losing ground. Protestors on Capital Avenue huddled in the rain. The professor with the sign and transparent raincoat had moved from his usual spot at the corner to the middle of the block. He gave me a quick salute. His pale legs and blue veins angered me. How easy to carry a sign; how easy to have a delusion.

Sharon's door stood ajar, even in the rain. Through the opening I saw the kitchen chair and table leg. Knocking, pushing on the door, my view widened to include Sharon seated on the landlord's—Steve's—sofa. The over-sized teddy bear beside her stared blankly at window glass steamed over from humidity. She got up. Taking the umbrella, she stepped to the tiny kitchen and hooked it over the oven door handle where it dripped onto the linoleum. I sat on the straight chair across from the sofa and studied the sodden purse lying on the carpet.

"Don't worry," she said. "It's only a toy."

I didn't know whether to believe her or not. I leaned forward. "I'd like to take the gun."

"I told you it's a toy." Seated beside the teddy bear again, she extended her foot and pushed the purse closer to me. I reached down, lifted the saturated flap, and peered inside. Grasping the butt and gingerly pulling the revolver up to daylight, I sat back and dangled it at arm's length. It was plastic, with no moving parts.

"Made in China," I read aloud.

"Your mother doesn't want to see you," Sharon said. "You're no different than me."

A gust of rain hit the east window. She uncrossed her arms and covered her eyes with those surprising hands, rough and competent. In a sudden eruption she cried, "Why won't he see me? He sees Roz. Why won't he see *me*?"

"He needs a mother now."

She took her hands down and braced herself on the edge of the sofa. "She told him to stop seeing me! I know she did. I know it." Sinking back onto the cushions, she shouted. "I hate her!"

I squeezed in next to the teddy bear and put one arm around her. "Roz can never be his mother," I said.

"She thinks she can. She thinks she *is*."

"She'll never be his mother," I repeated. "He will never have a mother."

Beads of tears rolled down her face. The stormy light fell over the three of us: Sharon, me, and the teddy bear. Patient rain nosed about the window glass for a way in.

"Roz says she can arrange a meeting with my mother," I said. "I'm going to bring my mother across the street to live with me."

Sharon rested her head on the back of the sofa. "Yeah. That's *your* motorcycle-and-gun plan."

I was silenced.

"Face it," Sharon said. "It won't work."

"My mother's old," I said. "They might let her out. She's troubled. I can help her."

"Yeah," said Sharon. "Tim's troubled, too, and they're not letting *him* out." The silence, the prison down the street, the Tuesday before Wednesday, absorbed us. Eventually Sharon went to the kitchen for my umbrella. "Good luck." I checked her eyes for sarcasm but found none. As soon as the door closed behind me, I started for Roz's house. I stepped over puddles and waves of dirt that had washed across sidewalks from roiled lawns. Mrs Winthrop's front yard looked as disturbed as everyone else's.

At Cherry Street I turned right and didn't pause until I met Trixie at the mailbox. After a regal stretch, the cat turned and escorted me indifferently up the wet porch steps.

Roz opened the screen door. Dressed to go out, she looked terrible. The bold print blouse and bright scarf made a public pronouncement that fought with her sad, inward face. I thought of the scars under her clothes and the channels and nodes where lymph slowed to sludge.

"Can you help me see my mother?" I blurted.

She didn't seem surprised. "Whenever you're ready, I'll talk to Ezekiel."

"You're not going to arrange it yourself?"

"Ezekiel is the person to ask." She studied me, then flung one end of the scarf over her shoulder. "Be available." She negotiated the rain-slick steps and swept toward her Lincoln parked in the driveway.

As instructed, I stayed near the telephone and my living room window overlooking the street. I kept an eye out for a dark green car going through elaborate parking motions at the curb. I waited for labored footsteps climbing the outside staircase. When I couldn't bear the tension any longer, I took a quick stroll past the prison before almost running the two blocks south on Cherry Street to Roz's, where I didn't find anyone at home and so immediately hurried back to the apartment in case she was looking for me.

Finally the telephone rang. "Be at my house at three," Roz said. "Pastor Schmidtke will reach the prison at three-thirty. We'll enter the same way we did on Sunday."

The only difference between Sunday and today was that Ezekiel was waiting for us. As I followed Roz's broad back through the high double doors of the prison entrance, on to the security stations, down the green hallway, and into the classroom, he walked alongside her. When we reached the classroom, I felt his eyes on me. He was the one person in the prison, Roz had told me, who my mother talked to.

"I know what you want," he said, approaching. "Follow me."

I looked at him sharply. "Please… " I meant "Please wait. I'm not ready."

Roz bent over her desk, her back to us. "Go," she whispered fiercely, and motioned with her hand while keeping her attention on the desk top. The guard in the hallway was looking the other way.

"Please, not yet," I said, but my legs and feet were already out the door and moving along the corridor. It occurred to me that perhaps I was as demented as my mother had been, thinking I was following God or Jesus when in reality I was only following Ezekiel.

His shoulders were wide. He walked slowly and powerfully, without any grinding of joints. He looked so at home, so comfortable and relaxed, that it was difficult to remember he was being punished or to imagine him as a young man milling about the prison yard in a sullen wash of male discontent. During a prison riot he'd been a ringleader, Roz had told me, and was tortured afterwards in "the hole," a basement cell in O-Hall.

I lagged behind. All the guards seemed to be somewhere else as I followed him across the main yard. Ezekiel swung back the gate to the hangar-sized limestone building.

"She's waiting on 6-Walk. She knows you're coming."

I followed him up several flights of steel steps, more like ladders than stairs. I climbed slowly. My mind quieted and my feet knew what to do.

A-Hall had catwalks stacked ten or more levels high, from floor to ceiling, along the four walls. A few guards walked back and forth on these platforms, though most of the levels seemed empty and unpatrolled. On the opposite side of the hall three or four old men lay on cots, eerily silent. Most cells were abandoned. From somewhere deep in the building I heard two TVs tuned to different channels, two soap operas, as if there were no news occurring just a few steps away where the gas chamber had been recently unlocked and cleaned.

On 6-Walk no one questioned why I was following Ezekiel. No one seemed to notice we were there. The cells we passed on this side were empty. Cots with stained mattresses lay in weak sunlight. One dirty quilt had been left behind. In the cavernous space, the sound of Ezekiel's footsteps flew up to the ceiling before falling back to ground-level. I wondered if he was required to wear shoes that rang against steel. One cell door just ahead on 6-Walk was ajar, out of alignment with the others. Ezekiel stopped in front of it. I had the odd wish to comb my hair. I did, in fact, re-tuck my shirt into my slacks. My mind stilled, as if I were about to meet myself.

Ezekiel stepped aside and I entered the cell. An old woman sat on the edge of the bed, bracing herself with both arms against the mattress. The arms were weak. Her ankles were crossed. Skinny, cotton-trousered knees pointed away from each other, spread apart in the way that aging women's legs sometimes fall open. The skin of her neck was as wrinkled as cloth puckered by a pulled thread. Two combs decorated with rhinestones held white hair at the crown of her head. When she lifted her head and looked at me, I knew her.

"Mother?" I whispered. I knelt by the cot and placed my

hands over hers. I moved our hands to the thin knees. She drew her legs together and leaned forward, touched my hair, cupped my chin. I looked up into her face.

"Evelyn," she whispered. Years fell away.

Faint, I laid my head on her lap. She smelled clean. I had expected otherwise. I looked up at Ezekiel who was standing by the cell door. I guessed that he was the one who kept her clean; the one who gave her rhinestone combs.

I began to shake; we were both shaking; I helped her lie down. She wept. Then her expression flattened to blankness. I stood beside the cot and held one of her hands. Ezekiel stepped forward and spread a blanket over her, then stepped back out again. Her gray eyes warmed once.

"Are you well these years?" I finally asked. My language sounded stilted.

"I've been well."

"Have you been here all this time?"

My mother nodded and gestured toward Ezekiel who watched from the open cell door.

"She worked in the hospital ward," he said. "They kept her here."

"They let me stay." My mother cleared her throat. She seemed unused to speaking. "I think Daddy talked to the Governor." She pulled hard on my hand which brought me down to a sitting position on the edge of the cot. Her voice was harsh. She cleared her throat but couldn't clear her voice. "Have you seen Daddy?"

My stream of tears cut deeply. Had no one told her that her husband was dead? "I saw him at Grandma and Grandpa's," I sobbed. "In the parlor." As soon as I pronounced it, the parlor exploded into life, like a concentrate in water. "He sat on Grandma's love seat," I added, and endured a spasm of joy while this stranger and I assembled Grandma's furniture, fringed cushions, fruit bowl from our common memory.

"No one visited me," she said.

I stared at the floor. My own foot and leg came in and out of focus. I was aware of my mother's hand moving along my arm, back, hair. "I'm sorry," I said. "I'm so sorry." I looked over at the window. Through the bars I tried to find our house, but the house was not in view.

"Our house, Mother. I'm living in our house just across the street."

Her face was flat with lack of interest. Slowly it developed contour. "Tell me if you married," she asked. "Do you have children?" She half-lifted her head from an improbable ribbon-edged pillow case that matched a sheet with pink polka-dots.

I adjusted one of the rhinestone combs. "My husband died last summer. We have a son and daughter." Her head sank back onto the pillow.

"When can I see my grandchildren?"

"Do you want to see them?"

She nodded.

I didn't say *but you wouldn't see me* because I was afraid I might break down, or scream, or pick up a framed snapshot and hit her with it. How good it would feel to get even, and how impossible.

Ezekiel stepped out onto the catwalk, one hand curled around a bar in the door as he stared down into A-Hall's cavernous space.

"Perhaps you could visit me across the street some day," I said. "Would you like that?" I touched one of the combs again. "Perhaps you could come across the street and live with me."

My mother stopped my hand. "What are the children's names?"

"Phyllis and Matthew."

"Phyllis and Matthew," she said.

"They can visit us in Jefferson City. There's room for all of us. I'm living on the second floor of our house," I rushed on. "One person can sleep in my old room. Two people can sleep in the guest room. We can set up a cot in the walk-in closet. And there's still your bedroom." My mother dropped my hand and turned toward the wall. "Your bedroom is the living room now," I added.

"Where do Matthew and Phyllis live?"

I would have preferred to talk about the house across the street. "California," I said.

"California," my mother repeated.

I looked about. Was the cell hers? Whether she lived here or had been brought for this meeting, I didn't know. She could hardly have climbed the steep stairs to the sixth level. Perhaps there was an elevator somewhere in the building. Or perhaps Ezekiel had carried her. She'd said she was well, but I didn't think so. She looked much older than seventy.

"Does she stay here?" I asked Ezekiel who was standing on the catwalk.

"Sometimes. When she does, I sleep close by. Her cell is in the old ward."

There were books on the single shelf, a water color propped against the wall, a photograph of my mother seated at the piano in our house across the street. On the bed, under the satin-edged pillow case, the pink polka-dot sheet was crisp and clean. Pillows of various sizes and colors softened the wall alongside the cot. There was a small table and reading lamp with a thick orange extension cord snaking out between bars and down the catwalk.

I swept the cell with my arm. "Do they let you do all this?"

Ezekiel stepped back into the cell and bowed modestly.

"He's a marvel," my mother said. I recognized the word. I'd often heard my mother use "a marvel" to describe something wonderful. There were two more photographs on the window ledge under the narrow, barred window. I couldn't make them out. Sliding a potted philodendron and its doily to one side, Ezekiel picked them up by their frames and handed them to me. One was himself as a young man, fiercely handsome, angry, formidable. The other was the Grant family standing in front of Miss Jaeger's piano studio. I wore the taffeta recital dress my mother had sewn at the Singer in the closet. All three of us looked happy. I felt sorry for us, so unaware of the future. I handed them back.

I wasn't ready to leave. I would never be ready to leave. But my mother and Ezekiel seemed ready for me to leave. Perhaps there was a limit to how much the rules could be broken. Perhaps they wanted to be alone together. I felt both of them pull away from me. Ezekiel stepped onto the catwalk.

"I don't want to go," I said, crying again and looking down at my mother.

"But you must, Evelyn."

Ezekiel returned to the cell and touched my shoulder, ready to escort me away. I shook him off. I wanted to spend the rest of my life in this cell.

"Remember how you used to read to me?" I said, grasping at something, anything, to talk about. Never mind that, as a child, I'd seen those grey eyes empty out during a story; had heard the most important voice in the world jump the narrative track and fall into a far-away sing-song. A poem or Bible verse being read by my mother was fluent but could become as blank as her gaze. Sitting on that lap, lolling under the arm that would soon cease to protect me, I'd followed my mother into opacity and blankness, though it was never long before I slid to the floor and found something real to touch: a doll, a ball, a Crayon.

"Remember how you used to read to me?" I repeated.

She failed to respond.

"Let me tell you about the house," I said, desperate to gain her attention. "The downstairs is pretty much the same, except the dining room is a library now and the new table from Milo Waltz is gone. Do you know what happened to it?"

But I saw that nothing about the house across the street interested her.

"And upstairs, they've made the sun porch into a kitchen."
Nothing.
"Mother?"

Her cheeks pinked. There was a rising force that gave shape to her face again. I held my breath because I thought she was going to say something about our house; our past; *me*. Her expression established itself. "You must leave," she said. "Obey me." No one had said that to me in forty years.

I kissed her good-bye, stood, and walked out of the cell. Half-blind from crying, I stepped onto the catwalk.

Ezekiel followed, leaving the door slightly ajar behind him. "I'll be back in a few minutes," he said, which made me intensely jealous. Then he was ahead of me, leading me back to the classroom. I saw no one as we returned. The visit had been neatly planned and executed.

Twelve

At five-thirty a.m. Wednesday, the day of the execution, I slipped into cool, loose clothing and descended the outside staircase. The overnight rainstorm had cleaned the world. My mother was just a few steps north; I would find a way to bring her the few steps south. Once outside the walls, once in her old home again, she would become herself and find happiness as a mother, grandmother, and soon, great-grandmother. Surely the administrators would be glad to have me take the only woman in the prison off their hands. She must be an awkward fact, too old to be incarcerated. I would talk to the Governor if necessary. *The prison will soon be moved*, I would say. *Now is a good time to dislodge her. Now is the right time to help her adapt to the world outside the walls. Now is the time for her to cross the white line in the middle of Capitol Avenue and come home.*

Stepping onto the sidewalk, I felt a vegetable-fresh breeze on my face. Bearing the scent of moist dirt and grass, it roamed freely, fragrantly, through the streets of Jefferson City. This was a morning from childhood when the fiery sunrise warms your back and the pink sky draws you forward into a pearly life filled with promise.

I crossed High. Downhill behind me a few demonstrators with tired voices began singing "Jesus, Savior, pilot me over life's tempestuous sea." The music faded as I neared the 24-hour coffee shop south of High. I'd brought a book; the newspapers in front of the restaurant would be obsessed with the execution.

Unlike Tim, my mother was safe. Long ago the State had decided not to execute Mabel Grant. Everyone knew she'd been misguided by a voice that wasn't God's. She'd thought it was God's, but it wasn't. Or if He'd actually spoken, He'd been wrong. Perhaps the church had given her inaccurate information on how God communicates and no one had corrected the mistake.

By the time my coffee was served, I'd closed the book and laid it on the table; I was too agitated to read. If Matthew and Phyllis in California knew about Tim Anguin, had somehow heard about what was happening at the Missouri Penitentiary, they would be worried and humiliated. It was two hours earlier in California; I would call them later today and tell them there was a chance their grandmother would be paroled and placed in my custody. I would tell them how eager she was to see them.

Thrilled at the prospect of a family reunion, veering between ecstasy and doubt about the future, I paid for my uneaten breakfast and began walking back to town. In a stand of trees beside one of the fine old South Side homes, a woodpecker's muted scream split the morning. Farther down the block, wisteria flowed over a fence like lavender water, sheltering fat, furry bees hanging upside down among the blossoms, humming with self-assurance as they lifted petals with neat efficiency to crawl underneath.

On High Street, Steve was just coming out of the religious supplies store. I crossed toward his pickup truck.

"That bouquet looks dangerously close to the flame, don't you think?" he said, studying his purchase, a recording whose cover showed candles burning beside a floral arrangement. A Bible lay open to a purple velvet bookmark. "Every now and then I enjoy a familiar old hymn." His lean face looked smudged this morning. Though his hair was combed, his shirt collar crisp, there was something rumpled about him. "Want to take a drive?"

We climbed into his pickup parked at the meter and drove west on High. "I've got to get out of Jeff City," he said. "The nervousness in the air... "

"I feel it, too," though it was excitement I felt. As we passed the stately old Sugarbaker home at the edge of town, now crowded by a Catholic Church and convent on one side, new houses on the other, I turned and confided in him. "I saw my mother yesterday."

"Oh?"

"She remembers me."

"I should hope so."

"It didn't last long." I didn't want to admit that she'd asked me to leave before I was ready to go.

"If anything," he said, "prison makes people worse."

Is she worse now than when she entered prison? I wanted to ask. "Did you ever hear any talk about my mother?"

"Nothing you don't already know."

I wondered how much he thought I knew. "I'm going to bring her across the street to live with me," I said.

He moved one hand to the stick shift.

"I'll get her paroled or something."

"Have you looked into it?"

"Well, no. It's still premature." The word "premature" had a deliberate, objective ring.

"You'll want to contact the Parole Board. It's changed since the new Governor came in."

We reached pastures and grazing cattle. Steve down-shifted and turned onto a county highway that took us to a shaded creek crossing. He parked the truck and we walked down the bank. Water running over stones murmured companionably.

"The creek's high after the rain," he said. "See these dirt breaks? They keep the road from washing out." He made a sweeping gesture with one arm. "You're in Lewis and Clark country."

"My mother can be released from prison, don't you think?" I said. "After all, she's old. She's been there a long, long time. She's a model prisoner."

Squatting easily, he tossed a twig in the water and watched it carried downstream. "That stick will end up in the Missouri," he said. Still watching it glide out of sight, he stood. "Does your mother want to be paroled?"

"Oh, I'm sure she does." We walked back to the truck. "Who would want to stay in prison if they didn't have to?"

He studied the sky before we got back in the pickup and followed the rutted road. Stopping at a metal gate, he climbed down from the truck, unlocked the padlock, pushed the gate on its hinges until it rested at the side of the road, and got back in. He drove forward a few feet and reversed the process. Approaching his property, he pointed to a line of birds walking out of the trees ahead. "Wild turkeys. Hens. Listen." I heard their cry before they disappeared into the trees again. I looked over at Steve's profile. He was completely absorbed in the woods.

No, not completely. "I can't shake the execution," he was saying. "I know every inch of the penitentiary. I've done work on the gas chamber." He shook his head slowly. "I wasted a lot of years. Sometimes you feel like you're living behind the walls, yourself." But, engineer that he was, he soon began talking about the physical plant. "The gas chamber is a little stone house close to your end of Capitol Avenue."

I leaned toward the window to catch any breeze moving through the woods.

"It's built to last. It's even plumbed. People in extreme situations lose control of bodily functions. They had to put a bathroom in the chamber. One execution was delayed an hour because the guy couldn't leave the stool."

I pictured Tim Anguin on his knees, clinging to a rusty iron toilet, vomiting, or sitting and moving his bowels while eternity rolled toward him. Here is death and the man has to pay attention to his last excretions.

"They used to hang people in a hayfield. Everyone in town came out to watch."

"I could use some fresh air," I said. We got out of the truck and slowly kicked through fallen leaves.

"Maybe you should see a lawyer about your mother's parole," he said. He paused to point out where deer rubbed their antlers against trees in the fall. Buck rubs, he called them. "Do you know the facts of the case?"

"I know what she did. I know she's been in prison for forty years."

At the base of the rise where the farmhouse stood, he pulled a gummy nest off a tree branch and scraped his fingers clean on the trunk. "Web worms in the hickory tree," he said, brushing his hands together matter-of-factly. We climbed the hill to the house. "Loose Creek flows along the far side of the property," he said, pointing. "The French called it Bear Creek. You can still see it on maps. Don't ask me how it got from "Bear" to "Loose.""

"'*L'ourse*' means 'the bear' in French," I said. "Maybe settlers thought the French were saying "loose."" He listened, interested. At the house I sat down on the porch. Inside, he was opening doors and windows on the ground floor. I heard him go upstairs and come down again.

"There's not much to do around here," he apologized, leaning against the door jamb, "except sit or work."

I stood up. "Put me to work." I followed him through the living room and dining room into the kitchen at the back of the house. It was a light, sunny room, all the brighter for having no curtains. The flooring had been stripped to the boards.

"Do you feel like laying tile?"

"Show me what to do."

He scanned the corners of the kitchen. "I've got extra knee protectors somewhere around here."

When he came back from the mud room, he was holding a second pair. We began crawling about the floor, laying tan-and-white tiles, working at an even pace. Around noon he took venison chili from the freezer and heated it on the propane stove. Work had given us an appetite. While the meat-and-beans aroma drove out the gluey smell of the new floor, we grated cheese and onions into bowls.

"I hate going back to town," he said. "I don't suppose you'd like to stay over? There are three extra bedrooms upstairs."

I hesitated. Sharon, alone at midnight tonight, crossed my mind. Roz's suffering crossed my mind. My toothbrush crossed my mind: I hadn't brought one. "How do you wash up?"

"Sparingly. I bring water from town."

Steve put his hands in his pockets, leaned against the stove, and watched me wipe out the chili pan with an old newspaper. "I wonder how long my renter will stay in town. She hasn't given notice."

"She visited me on Monday and slept over," I said.

"She slept over?"

"She was upset. She fell asleep on my air mattress. She left before I could give her breakfast."

"Did she talk about Tim Anguin?"

"Not much. She's in love with him. He won't see her." I inspected the inside of the pan.

"Go ahead and wash it," he said. "Sparingly."

"She had a couple of hare-brained plans for rescuing him. I imagine by now she's accepted the facts."

"She's so young," he said. He stared at the line where the new tiles met the subfloor. "Why her parents let her stay here alone is beyond me."

"She's strong," I said. "A strong teenager."

"That young?"

"I think so."

"Does Roz know about her?"

"Oh, yes. Yes, indeed, they know each other. And there's no love lost." I told him about the visit, omitting the graphic details of the bikini. He waited for me to say more. "Both of them want to be the only woman in Tim Anguin's life," I added. "The man knows how to keep them competing."

Steve moved away from the stove. "Aren't you being a little hard on him?"

I lifted my hands, palms up. "I don't know. Do you think it's possible to be too hard on him?"

He led the way into the living room. A damp breeze had begun to blow. Through the open windows I felt rain approach. What would it be like to smell rain, knowing it's the last time you'll breathe that moist, tweedy scent or feel its slanting needles?

God bless Tim Anguin. God bless Sharon.

"Well, we all have our troubles," Steve said, easing himself into a walnut rocking chair by the window. He executed a couple of short arcs against the old boards. "Mine are small in comparison." There was an interval of silence. "My cousin is making my uncle's last years miserable," he said. "She's making my last years miserable, too."

"I doubt these are your last years, Steve."

He shrugged. "Who knows?"

"Can't you prove her wrong? You have financial records, don't you?"

"Oh, yeah. It's the cost of a lawyer, the misery of going to court that I don't want. It's the hostility." His usual reticence, lodged in few words, precise movements, even in the creases of his face, deserted him. "What bothers me is that she makes me feel sorry for my uncle. He was always a fair-minded guy. It embarrasses him to have his daughter accuse me of stealing. At first it embarrassed me, too. But it doesn't embarrass me anymore. It pisses me off." He leaned sharply forward. The rocker came to an abrupt stop. "She's jealous. She wanted to manage his finances, but he asked me, instead. I resent her for dragging him into a family fight in his last years." He took another sharp back-and-forth and looked restlessly through the window at the stormy sky. "Maybe I should have said no." Without warning, he stood. "The kitchen floor won't dry anytime soon in this weather. Still, I think I'll put down a few more tiles."

I moved to the rocking chair he'd vacated. My mother told me once that, as a girl, she would sit in her parents' farmhouse on days like this, listening to the wind, smelling a storm, hoping the wheat crop wouldn't be hailed out. In the yellowish-green light, I watched the leaves blow upside-down on their branches and imagined my mother as a child.

"Do you know how to use a stick shift?" Steve called from the kitchen.

"Certainly," I called back. "I lived with my grandparents on a farm in Idaho. I drove all the time."

"Would you bring the truck up to the house?"

After a short walk I reached the pickup where we'd left it and climbed into the driver's seat. I didn't need to look at the diagram incised into the knob of the stick. I knew the shift pattern as well as I'd known my grandparents' farm. Clutch down. Wiggle the stick in neutral. Shift left, then forward into first. My mind slipped back thirty-some years. I was leaving for school. I had early choir practice today. Or maybe it was Saturday and Grandma and I were going to shop in town.

Clutch, down. Shift into second. Maybe I was going to pick up my grandfather from the field. I drove him there early in the morning because I needed the truck for town. Now I'm bringing him back to the house for supper. Before Grandma tells me to help her in the kitchen, I'll go to the out-of-tune upright in the corner of the parlor and plunk out a Bach phrase I remember from Miss Jaeger's piano lessons. But I can't remember the whole thing, and anyway, my grandmother doesn't like for me to play the piano when there's work to do. There's always work to do. *"Come stir the gravy for me, Evelyn,"* she calls from the kitchen. It's milk gravy. Seventy-five percent of our dinners were fried chicken, mashed potatoes, and milk gravy.

Steve's truck wanted to stall. I dropped back into first, crawled up the gravel drive to the house, and parked. From the lip of the hill I looked down at the woods dappled in shifting light. The sound of tree limbs sighing and creaking rose through the damp air.

My grandparents, along with Steve, Sharon, Roz, Tim

Anguin, seemed present in the light and in the woods; my mother was the weather itself.

When I returned to the house, Steve was unbuckling his knee guards and stacking the remaining tiles in the corner. "Think I'll give the old back a rest." He bent from side to side, straightening out kinks. "Anything in particular you want to do?"

"What would you be doing if I weren't here?"

"Cutting up the tree that fell near the road"— he looked out the window—"before it rains."

"I'll help." He threw a chain saw and ax into the truck bed and we jounced away, forking off the gravel road into the woods behind the house. He worked hard cutting branches and the trunk into logs while dark clouds blowing across the sun made the light come and go. I set the big logs on end and, after some tentative strokes, split them in two. We tossed the split logs and kindling into the bed of the truck.

"You'll be warm this winter." I'd admired the woodburner in the living room, its shiny black body, bright brass fittings, glass door.

"You bet," he said.

Back at the house we unloaded the wood and stacked it in the mudroom. It was five o'clock. We sat down again in the living room. Steve rocked a few times in the chair. I took off my shoes, stretched out my legs, and set my stocking feet on the coffee table.

"How old are your kids?" he asked.

"Twenty-five and twenty-eight."

"Do they—" He was going to ask how much they knew about their grandmother. I could feel the question as he was forming it. "Children are a wonderful thing," he said, veering off, "especially when they're good kids."

"Yes."

"I guess you were married a long time."

"Long time."

He checked his watch. "When I think about what Tim Anguin's going through tonight, I guess I should count my blessings." He rocked. "I'll admit my life has disappointed me in certain respects."

"Oh?"

"Yeah. Three areas. My job. My marriage. My home."

What else was there?

"I haven't broken any frontiers. I'm living on the same patch of ground where my parents lived. You remember the house."

"I remember it well. But you've built an apartment building," I said. "It may be the same patch of ground, but you've made something new out of it."

"Do you like the building?" The question was touchingly frank.

"Yes," I said. "It updates the neighborhood. It's kind of—what would you call it—a counterweight to the prison. God knows we need a counterweight."

"Yep," he said. "Good word."

Conversation grew more and more desultory. Soon we were taking cat naps in our chairs, starting out of sleep with embarrassed apologies and jokes about getting old. Evening approached. The next bowl of chili, dinner, wasn't as good as the first.

"What time is it?" I asked when he'd taken the garbage to the compost and I'd hung up the dish towel.

"Seven."

We moved from the kitchen into the living room again. Steve began drumming his fingers on the chair arm. "No TV," he apologized. Eventually we moved out onto the porch and watched the sun lower itself to the horizon where it hesitated, postponing night. Postponing midnight.

"Which bedroom should I take?" I asked just before daylight ended.

"The bed to the left of the landing is made up."

I climbed the staircase. Bending over the bed, I folded back the quilt and top sheet. The last of the sunset was stormy, unreliable, murky red. Through the rippled glass of the old window I could see the barn below. The timeless slant of its roof was matter-of-fact. Beyond it, out to the sunset, stretched the woods. I kicked off my shoes and lay down on the bed.

I awoke to scratching in the wall. At least I hoped it was in the wall. I moved; the scratching stopped. I lay still; it resumed. Something was listening.

The scratching intensified. It grew louder and gained speed. Its friction was rougher than my pulse and far more rapid. Now when I moved, it didn't stop to listen; it scratched faster. It was the sound of everything that lives and wants to continue living. Finally, while I held my breath, the tiny engine revved itself to its highest possible pitch—I couldn't imagine anything faster—and the creature broke through something and abruptly grew silent.

Oh, God, where was it? I moved, even bounced slightly, on the mattress. But the scratching had died. I sat up, slid into my shoes, and tiptoed down the stairs. Just as I reached the front door, Steve spoke from the chair next to the woodburner: "Can't sleep?"

I jumped. "There was a mouse or something in the wall."

"I should have warned you about that."

I pushed the screen door open. "What time is it?"

"Eleven-fifteen."

I walked to the outhouse. The night had turned balmy and dry. The moon was at three-quarters. Its incompleteness made me anxious. When I returned I sat down in the chair beside Steve's. I could make out his white shirt in the darkness.

"It never did storm," he said.

Capitol Avenue would be crowded now, loud with scriptures, hymns, and prayers. The gas chamber would be brightly lit and open for business. There would be officials and Reverend Schmidtke. And there, off to the side, would be Tim Anguin, bent over the iron toilet, emptying himself. I imagined Sharon and Roz at the moment of his death, hot tears flash-frozen on their cheeks. Later I learned they had actually stood outside the prison, leaning against each other, touching the wall from the street side at midnight.

Love for Tim overcame their personal animosity, Roz told me after it was all over. She and Sharon had cried at the wall. Trembled. The trembling was unbelievable, she told me, like a strange illness. Like being sick in the tropics. After the courthouse clock struck twelve, a uniformed officer told them to go home. Roz walked Sharon to her studio apartment, then returned to the house on Cherry Street, full of a voluminous weightlessness, she said, that lifted her while keeping her feet securely on the sidewalk. She felt bereft and supported at the same time. She knew Tim was her son in every respect and that he'd loved her, then shaken her off because he didn't need her anymore. When, early the next morning, she'd walked back to Sharon's apartment to make breakfast, the girl had already packed her bags and left town. Roz found her car parked in the next block.

"How did she get home?" Roz wondered aloud. "Did she take a bus?"

"Tim's motorcycle," I said, and described Sharon buzzing toward the Ozarks, her dead boyfriend's spirit riding along with her. Roz listened, doubtful.

"It happened once before when she drove the Harley to her parents' house," I said, throwing in supporting facts. "She rode it from Kansas City at night, south and east, to her parents' house where she hid it under a tarp. But her father found it, so she rode it back here and hid it in the woods behind Capitol Avenue." I stopped, proud of having so much authentic information.

"By the way, where were you Wednesday night?" Roz asked.

I hesitated. "Not in Jefferson City."

Roz's gaze shifted a fraction of an inch away from eye contact. "Where were you?"

"On Steve's farm."

She looked disappointed in me. I was disappointed in me. I'd run away from difficulty. Run from the execution and from Sharon who could have used my support. Roz moved closer and patted my shoulder. "I stayed with Sharon. The two of us managed to get through it."

Now, a half hour before midnight, with his work shoes on the floor beside him, Steve leaned back in the chair and stretched his legs out in front of him. But he was restless and soon got up. The gas chamber was real to him, whereas my imagination colored the execution and protected me. He hooked his thumbs in the back pockets of his Levis and moved onto the porch in his stocking feet. I followed him to the bench where we sat and leaned against the house, sensing the original log cabin, the core of the building, behind us.

"The Pleiades," he said, studying the sky. "Venus. The Big and Little Dipper." He closed his eyes. "I always wanted a family." He cleared his throat. "I'm not good at relationships."

I felt a rush of gratitude to Walter for our years of happiness. Just as swiftly, I recognized they were over, like a shooting star one might see out here on Steve's farm. After it blazes and falls, the moon and stars continue on, refulgent, steady, reaching farmhouses and porches. But the blaze is over.

Steve reached for my hand and, together, we crossed the hallway into the bedroom. "I can't get the execution out of my mind," he said. He looked at his watch and sat down on the edge of the bed. I sat down beside him. His shoulder against mine was warm.

"On a night like this I can't stop thinking about Tim and the mistakes I've made," he said.

"Don't equate mistakes with crimes." I sounded too brisk for the circumstances. "We've all made mistakes."

The platitude didn't interest him. "Living on the same street as the State penitentiary humbles a person." Silence. "I'm not a relationship guy."

"I can't help pointing out, Steve, that you're sitting beside me on a double bed."

He smiled wanly. "Yeah, but I'm on the edge. And I'm sitting." He grew glum again. "My divorce set up a chain of events that are causing trouble to this day. My wife hated my cousin. They competed."

"Over you?"

"You could say that. It didn't help my marriage. Eventually we got the divorce, but it was tough there for a while."

"My husband," I said, "knew how to be married. I didn't. I was lucky with Walter."

"I'll feel better when tonight is over," he said after a while. "Capital punishment influences everything. The school reunion isn't going to happen. No one wants to celebrate anything. They read about Tim Anguin in the paper, and all those happily married people decide to stay home."

"All those people aren't happy, Steve. You're exaggerating." We dug into each other with our shoulders, two people on a bad night. Then we both exhaled. Steve put his arm around me. We lay back, cross-wise, on the bed. Soon we changed position so that our heads were on the pillows, our feet toward the footboard. We lay close, back to back. Steve's breathing was steady. I clung to the thought: we'll sleep well and wake up with the sun shining on our faces. God—something—someone— will care for Tim and Sharon and Roz.

During the night we woke once and made sleepy sounds without language. The next time I woke we were back to back again, stable, braced against each other.

Suddenly it was a new day. We'd lived through the night. Thursday was radiant. Steve was already up. I got out of bed and went into the kitchen, wondering what we would have for breakfast. The half of the floor that had been laid down looked fresh and clean in daylight. I knew the other half would be perfect, too, as soon as we finished it.

Thirteen

Time, forever digesting itself, produced Thursday, then Friday. I strayed, as usual, to Roz's house, where the luxury of imagining gave way to fact. Roz told me exactly what happened on the night of the execution.

"Sharon rang my doorbell before the execution, around ten, crying, just desperate," she said as we sat on her porch swing. "I found her huddled right there"—she pointed to the porch floor—"with her back against the railing. I all but picked her up and put her in the swing. We rocked back and forth like you and I are doing right now. Just before midnight we went up to the prison and stood at the wall. The officers didn't bother us. They knew who we were. She stopped crying and complained of the cold. I hugged her and tried to keep her warm"—Roz shook her head. "The temperature was in the 80s, you know, but we were both shaking. I didn't realize until the clock struck twelve that it was all over."

"It struck twelve?" I gave an automatic push against the floorboards. The swing regained momentum. "I've never heard the courthouse clock strike twelve midnight."

"Only on solemn occasions."

Trixie absentmindedly padded up the steps, preoccupied.

"Can you help with the literacy class next week, Evelyn?"

There it was. Roz never gave up.

"Are things already back to normal behind the walls?" I asked.

"Change becomes normal," she said. "When the going gets tough, Evelyn, the tough get going." The cat, who had thrown herself down in the corner, stretched out to a languid full-length and let her eyes glide back into her head.

"Okay," I said to Roz. "I'll help."

"Why don't you come for breakfast tomorrow morning and we'll go to the prison together."

When I crossed the porch next morning and entered the house on Cherry Street, breakfast was waiting.

"Things have quieted down," Roz announced as we salted and peppered our eggs. "Needless to say, everyone has been restless and disturbed, but we're going to make a new start. Can you bring me another napkin?" She dabbed at a spot of orange juice on her flowered scarf. "Of course, the inmates are still a little depressed, but the anger is gone. The horror has died down, too. It's not easy having a penitentiary in town." She rested her hand on mine. "I want to thank you for your afternoon at Vacation Bible School registration, and for coming to the prison with me the other day. I've been imposing on you, I know."

"I need to get a life," I said. "I was deteriorating, thinking only of myself." With a sideways glance—no, a visual slash—I caught sight of Roz's regal chin and nose. Profile of woman-strength. Cancer-survivor. Prison-teacher. Tim-comforter. Sharon-rescuer. Mother-finder. I admired her; I resented her.

"You haven't told me about your meeting with your mother," Roz said.

"Didn't we talk about that? Didn't Ezekiel tell you about it?"

"Nobody has told me anything."

"Some day," I said, "I'll tell you everything." Except for Steve, who never quizzed me, I was not going to share my mother with anyone. Anyway, there was pitifully little to share. My mother had sent me away. Most of the time her face had been blank. She'd displayed more interest in her grandchildren than in me. More interest in California than in our house across the street. So, no, I had nothing to tell Roz. I intended only one thing: to become a fixture in the prison. People would grow used to seeing me in the classroom and corridors. If your mother wants to stay in her cell, you have to go to the cell. With Ezekiel's help, dropping in on 6-Walk would become routine. There were few guards, and those that patrolled the cat-walks didn't seem to be really there.

But I had to start soon, before the prison closed.

"Can you pour us a little more coffee, Evelyn?"

Walter had been a thoroughly honest man. He'd been too honest for his own good. He never played the political games necessary to rise to the top levels of management. He'd possessed very little self-interest. He'd never had an ulterior motive in his life, and he would disapprove of mine. Of course, if he'd kept an eye out for traffic instead of reading while he was crossing the street, he'd still be alive and I wouldn't have to be here alone, stalking my mother through the ruins of the family home, sleeping on an air mattress in temporary rooms that had been closed up for years. If he'd looked both ways before he stepped off the curb, I wouldn't be here, relentlessly circling the Missouri State Penitentiary, trying to get inside a cell on 6-Walk.

"Nobody tells me anything," Roz repeated, but more matter-of-factly this time. She wiped her mouth with a napkin and got to her feet. "Shall we look over the books for class?" I heard the rocking chair in the living room creak. Through the kitchen window above the sink, the sky was bright blue at 8:00 a.m. The outdoor thermometer nailed to the window frame already said ninety degrees. The cool spell had ended as quickly as it began.

"Can you bring my coffee when you come, Evelyn?"

I delivered the coffee without any slop-over. Thin paperback books lay scattered on the low table beside Roz, stories filled with dire circumstances described in a controlled vocabulary for adults learning to read. One told about a fire in which a father saves his son after the firemen have failed. In another, a young employee locked inside the walk-in refrigerator of a fast-food restaurant rescues himself.

"I don't know anything about teaching prisoners," I said after I'd flipped through several stories of deliverance. Perhaps I, too, would be delivered from the literacy class. I would like that. I would like for Roz to terminate my services before they began. Release me from the role I'd recently assigned myself: subversive agent inside the prison.

She looked up from the copious notes she was making in large, loopy handwriting. "Oh, you won't find the morning difficult, Evelyn. Today you're just observing and listening to students read." She capped her ballpoint pen. "We'll have a writing lesson for the first forty minutes, then I'll give a short assignment and we'll help the students individually. After a break we'll listen to them read. For homework, they'll do a reader response. Simple. We want them to think about what they read and then express themselves. Class discussion can be lots of fun." She stood and left the empty chair rocking vigorously behind her. "What did I do with my car keys?"

"Aren't we walking?"

"Heavens, no."

Even though the guards knew Roz, she had to pass through the security equipment like everyone else. We stopped at the X-ray station. One of the corrections officers put the briefcase on the conveyor belt where it lay on its side like a fat pet that can't get up. Our drivers' licenses had already been turned in at the entrance. I followed Roz to the next stop, a desk where the briefcase was manually searched and the backs of our hands stamped with purple ink. It was the same routine we'd been through before.

I stayed near the guard as he escorted us to the classroom. "Are the prisoners in their cells now?" I asked, looking behind me.

"They're at work," he said.

I imagined shackled inmates filing through town, dropping away, one by one, to toil on construction sites, in businesses, restaurants, office buildings. This town, this little pond, this little ecosystem, was infiltrated by felons.

Roz looked at my face and laughed. "Evelyn, they work in the prison. They make things. Furniture for State offices. State seals. License plates. They don't work in town. The State factories are here."

"We used to have a private broom factory. Shoe factory, too," said the officer, motioning us toward the final visitors' gate.

"You know the white brick house a few doors from your house?" Roz asked me. "That's the old Carson house. Mr Carson had a broom factory and used prison labor for his production line."

"Was that legal?"

Roz and the guard laughed. "Back then it was."

I could trump them. I'd actually known Mr Carson. When I was a girl my father pointed him out at church and whispered, "He's a very rich man," just before the old gentleman bent stiffly at the waist, reached across the pew, and shook my hand. His brittle bones, fragile as a bird's, had formed a hollow between his thumb and index finger. Perhaps the pressure of broom handles had created that webbed notch.

I turned to Roz and said almost haughtily, "Once my family and the Carsons were invited to the Governor's Mansion for dinner. The Governor was my father's patient, you know. There was a trusty who served us. I remember being worried because he held the carving knife."

"The prisoners we'll be teaching don't have knives," Roz said, as if that had been the point of my story. Actually there had been no point to the story except the wish to pronounce my father and Mr Carson's names and to show that my Jefferson City credentials were as authentic as anyone else's. We followed the guard up one hall and down another. Men's voices deeper in the building echoed against the green cement-block walls. In the distance a metal gate clanged shut. We turned a corner and our escort unlocked the classroom.

Roz walked in and emptied her briefcase onto the desk. She asked me to arrange the students' chairs in a circle. "We used to meet in a larger room," she said as she wrote the date on the blackboard. "Through the years we've been shuffled from building to building." She sighed. "Soon we'll be moving again. For now, they're busing the men from the new site."

I was sorry to see the prison move. It had colored my childhood. My family had seemed more substantial, luckier than we actually were because we contrasted with the prison across the street. Sympathetic prayers for criminals, the drawing of the drapes each evening against the search lights, the righteous profiles of the guard towers against the sky, all had defined us. The limestone wall had shored up my sense of home and helped convince me I was a good person since the bad ones were on the other side.

A high, shrill bell rang. A half dozen men filed through the door, a mix of whites and African-Americans. The temperature in the room rose. The men were terribly physical. I had never attached real bodies to the idea of prisoners across the street. To me, they'd been souls my mother prayed for. Their actual heads, hands, shoulders, legs appalled me.

They had names. After Roz introduced them, the men sat down in one-armed chairs arranged in a circle. I joined them and they all turned to Roz for authority.

"I've missed you," Roz said. "We've been through a bad time." That was her only reference to Tim Anguin. She went right into the day's lesson. "Turn to page five."

The men followed her directions. They paid absolute attention to this heavy, misshapen woman from the other side of the wall who knew their names and was not frightened of their bodies. They barely noticed my presence. Teaching assistants, I sensed, came and went, and I was just one more volunteer in a long line of volunteers who let in quick gusts of fresh air before going away again, shutting the door behind them.

The reading lesson was based on a story, "Nat Welds Copper Rod," whose vocabulary restricted itself to the phonics system Roz taught. She wrote a sentence on the chalkboard that incorporated a list of related spelling words: "Nat," "hat," "held," "weld."

Seated next to each man in turn, hearing the expulsions

of breath as they pronounced the words, beginning to feel the weight of their shoulders in my own as they bent over their papers, I experienced a surprising tenderness. Beside me, a man named Tom diligently practiced writing his words. Ezekiel, on my other side, tutored the student to his left. I heard the rumble in his nasal passages, "n-n-n," then the flat "a-a-a" vowel, and finally the pop of the "t-t-t."

"Nat," he concluded in a deep, steady voice.

I looked at him sideways: man-killer, riot-maker, mother-guardian, prison teacher. Rival.

"Cop-per," I said, pointing to each syllable on Tom's paper. "Cop-per." "Weld-ing."

Wal-ter. My husband would be surprised to hear me pronounce his name inside a prison. I shook my head. *No, Walter, I won't be here much longer. Only until I get my mother back.*

Tom looked up. He thought he'd made a spelling mistake.

"I wasn't shaking my head at you, Tom. You've spelled it right." With his pencil poised above the next word, he'd been more aware of my thoughts than I of his.

After the break Roz read a poem by Robert Frost. She wrote the opening lines on the board and asked me to hand around copies of the entire poem. The first two lines were printed in bold. The men grasped their No. 2's in their thick hands and copied:

> *Some say the world will end in fire,*
> *Some say in ice.*

Roz asked me to join her in reading the two lines aloud. The men paid attention. They seemed interested in the end of the world.

"Read out loud with Evelyn and me," she said. They all read. The reading was fitful and arrhythmic. "Louder!" she demanded. Everyone read louder and better. When they'd memorized the two lines, Roz asked them to whisper the words. The men and I felt silly but followed directions. When they read out loud again, their voices flowed like honey.

"Punch it!" Roz said, and they hit each syllable with separate action. She asked Ezekiel to read the remainder of the poem. After more discussion and practice, the others joined him. The deep male voices wound through the lines. Some of the poorer readers dropped out. By the end, Ezekiel and two others were still in the game. They recited slowly.

> *Some say the world will end in fire,*
> *Some say in ice.*
> *From what I've tasted of desire*
> *I hold with those who favor fire.*
> *But if it had to perish twice,*
> *I think I know enough of hate*
> *To say that for destruction ice*
> *Is also great*
> *And would suffice.*

The back of my neck softened, bristled, and softened again. My skin comprehended the men and the poem. I looked at Roz; her throat was mottled red and her face was pale.

Immediately after the bell, I caught up to Ezekiel. "How is my mother today?" Behind me, Roz packed student papers into her briefcase.

"She's doing fine."

"Will you tell her hello for me?" The inadequacy of saying hello contrasted grievously with what I wanted to do: throw my arms around him, cry out, "Take me to her!" and confess into his neck how significant the visit to 6-Walk had been. How jealous I was that he could see her every day. How sorry I would be to steal Mabel Grant away from him.

"I certainly will do that, Mrs Williams."

"I'd like to see her again, Ezekiel."

"I can understand that."

But he didn't offer to take me to 6-Walk. Though he still stood respectfully in front of me, at any moment he would turn and go back to my mother while I would have no choice but to walk out of the prison with Roz. While my mother and Ezekiel talked quietly in the cell on 6-Walk, I would be back in the second floor of my old home, a cell of my own, sitting on a folding chair.

I held out one hand and begged. "Can't you take me to see her again?"

Under white eyebrows, his dark gaze alerted me to disappointment. "I would if I could."

"Why can't you?" I blurted.

He motioned to the corridor on the other side of the door and lowered his voice. "Special arrangements have to be made."

"Can't we at least plan for another visit? I'll be here helping in the classroom every day. I'll be ready anytime you say the word."

He shifted his weight and looked at my chin, my forehead, before returning to my eyes.

I would not cry in front of him. Ezekiel reached into his shirt pocket. Behind us, Roz latched her briefcase.

"Your mother sent you this," he said, and handed me a folded piece of white tablet paper. The thin red line of rubber ran along the top where she'd torn it off. I loved this remnant and her fingerprints I could not see. Roz approached. I folded the paper once more and tried to hold it casually, inconspicuously.

In the parking lot, she tossed the briefcase into the back seat and climbed in behind the steering wheel. When she turned on the engine, a blast of hot air from the air conditioner blew into our faces. She leaned back. "What do you think of the class?"

My mother's letter was a feather, a bowling ball inside my purse.

"I enjoyed the class. I like the men. It's hard to believe they committed crimes."

"Believe it, Evelyn."

"What did they do?"

"Rape, murder, armed robbery." She threw back her shawl. Tilting the rear view mirror toward herself, she fluffed her short, curly hair, checked her teeth for lipstick, then readjusted the mirror. The engine idled and the air conditioner hummed.

"Who did what?"

With aplomb Roz enumerated the men and their crimes.

"Ezekiel must have been a very different man when he was young," I said, expressing admiration for an obstacle I intended to dispense with. "He's not a criminal anymore. Don't they release people from prison if it's been years and years and they don't cause trouble? Don't they get 'good time'?"

"Oh, he's accumulated years of good time," Roz said.

I didn't ask about my mother's good time. There must be lots of it.

"He's intelligent," I continued. "He reads and writes well."

"He spends most of his free time in the prison library." Roz showed no interest in pulling out onto the street. We were parked under a magnificent oak that somehow flourished in cement. Its leaves occasionally fluttered, then lay flat again in the still day. Patches of tar around the roots gleamed and oozed in the hot sun. "Ezekiel could leave anytime, but he doesn't want to."

"Why not?"

"It's his only home." She shifted into reverse. Bearing down on both the accelerator and brake, she backed out of the parking space and clipped a curb with her left rear tire as she set sail across the parking lot. She followed an elderly, cautious driver in an ancient Cadillac whose taillights blinked on and off as he motored past rows of cars, unaware that the danger lay not in the open water ahead, but in the stop-and-go wake behind. Managing to avoid him, Roz crossed Capitol Avenue and dropped anchor at the apartment. Reaching into her purse, she pulled out a plain sheet of lined paper that was Scotch-taped into a sealed, make-shift envelope. "Sharon left this for you."

I registered surprise.

"Two letters in the same day," she added blandly. "I forgot to give it to you."

"When did she write it?"

"Wednesday night." She pressed the heels of her hands against her eyes. The quick change of emotion always caught me off-guard. "She was looking for you."

"Looking for me? But I thought you found her on your porch."

"She'd been to your apartment."

I hadn't been home. I felt the depth of Roz's service to others. "She found *you*," I said. Life-giver. Sharon-rescuer. Holding my purse in one hand, Sharon's letter in the other, I stepped out onto the pavement. The Lincoln lurched away from the curb and turned down Cherry Street. In the silence left behind, Capitol Avenue lay throbbing in the noon sun. Beside me, a bee floated up the outside staircase on a draft of air.

Bless the bees. I opened my door, passed through the brick wall, and continued on through the apartment. In the kitchen I turned on the air conditioner unit and moved one of the folding chairs directly in front of it. I propped the two letters against the sugar bowl on the counter and sat down. The breeze from the air conditioner fan brushed through my hair.

Sharon had been looking for me but I had been no-where in Jefferson City. I reached for her letter and picked at the tape. Eventually I needed a paring knife to slit open the handmade envelope.

> *Dear Evelyn,*
> *Tim died tonight. Jesus loves him. Jesus loves your mother and you just like he loves Tim and I. Good luck.*
> *Sharon Riley*

I hadn't known her last name. I waited a full minute and opened my mother's letter.

> *Dear Evelyn,*
> *I am very sorry I cannot see you. Your visit left me*
> *so sad and upset that I cannot see you again. Please*
> *understand.*
> *All my love,*
>   *Your Mother*

I re-read the small, precise handwriting I'd seen forty years earlier in a three-ring binder labeled *"Methodist Circle: Sacred Literature Club."* Too, there had been the notes to Miss Schroer, Mrs Guyot, Miss Benninghoff: *"I have read Evelyn's report card and discussed it with her. Thank you. Mabel Grant." "I will be picking Evelyn up early today for a special event with her piano teacher. Thank you. Mabel Grant."*

Still sitting in front of the air conditioner, I read my mother's letter one more time. Then I walked to the bathroom, tore the letter into tiny pieces, and flushed it down the toilet. The sewer accepted it. My mother could rot in jail. Ezekiel could keep Mabel Grant and so could the State of Missouri.

But that night, kneeling on the floor of the walk-in closet, I ground my forehead into the floorboards. My mother and I must not shut ourselves away, the mother for life, the daughter for a summer. We must get out. We must do something. Be like Roz in the world. Be like Sharon. A letter must go out.

> *Dear State of Missouri:*
> *I will be removing my mother from 6-Walk.*
> *Thank you.*
> *Evelyn Grant Williams.*

> *Dear Ezekiel,*

I will be freeing my mother from your clutches.
Thank you.
Evelyn Grant Williams.

Undressing for bed, brushing my teeth, creaming my face—a silly gesture, now that Walter was dead, who cared if I had wrinkles?—I made plans to talk to the prison officials. I would bring my grown children—my mother's grandchildren, the secret weapon she could not resist—to Jefferson City. I would string Ezekiel along and use him to communicate with my mother. Finally, I would dislodge him from Mabel Grant's affections; otherwise, there was no room for me to curl up in the center of her heart where I belonged. With Walter gone, there was nowhere else to rest.

Fourteen

"Would you get spoons for the oatmeal?" Roz had made breakfast again. Quiet through most of the meal, she suddenly stood up from the table and burst into tears.

God, I thought, jumping up, too. What now?

"Chew," I said, worried about the simultaneous crying, sniffing, and swallowing.

"My ex-husband is very ill," she said brokenly, adding speech to the other moist functions.

"Where is he?"

"St. Louis." She pulled at her tank top that lay under her partially buttoned blouse and silk scarf. "His brother called me early this morning. Simon has cancer!" She spat out the word and shook herself like a dog. "I hate cancer! If he dies I'll lose him all over again!" Her voice unraveled and she whispered, "I always thought he would fall in love with me again. We were so powerful and sexual together." She limped into the living room. I followed as she settled into the rocking chair and began oscillating fiercely.

"Is he in the hospital?"

"Yes. All this time he's been sick. No one told me. No one tells me anything!"

I pulled a straight chair next to the rocker. "But you've been divorced for many years, haven't you?"

"Only twenty." She could not forget Simon. She didn't like being excluded or, worse, forgotten. I laid a hand on the chair arm to stop her compulsive rocking.

"Roz," I said as gently as I could, "I'm afraid if we don't leave now we're going to be late for class."

"Can you start without me, Evelyn? I'll be there in a few minutes."

Teach alone? I began to perspire. Lead a class of prisoners? But I got my purse and stepped out onto the porch.

Bracing myself against the heat, I walked briskly toward Capitol Avenue. Cardinals called from tree to tree along Cherry Street, their bright red movements punctuation marks to the class exercise I was trying to devise in my head.

When I was finally escorted through the security gates and corridors, I found twelve men and one corrections officer waiting in the classroom. They looked disappointed when I, instead of Roz, walked in. I went straight to the board and wrote her name, then underneath it, in smaller print, my own. I asked everyone to introduce themselves. The jumble of spoken syllables washed over me. I would never remember their names.

"On Monday we read 'Fire and Ice,'" I began. "Roz—Ms Teal—will be here before long with copies. In the meantime"—I faltered, incapable of discussing with criminals what Robert Frost might mean when he talks about the world ending in fire; in ice. If anyone knows fire, it's murderers and rapists. Passion. Anger. Guns. And ice? Armed robbers. Cold and calculating. And the end of the world? When Tim Anguin dragged his ankle chains to death row, that was the end of the world. Whenever the foreman of a jury says "Guilty"… No, I was not going to discuss fire and ice today.

Their dubious expressions were turning into amusement.

"Until Ms Teal gets here," I said, "I'm going to ask you to fill in a missing word."

Two of the men terrified me. One, with a diagonal slash across forehead, eye, and cheek, was as sinewy as barbed-wire. The other, angry-eyed, had forced his bulk into a student desk from which I feared he would never extricate himself. His fat and muscle were interlarded in a brutal display of marbled weight.

Bless the prisoners.

"The sixth month of the year is… " They looked puzzled, then contemptuous.

"Welcome to Kindergarten," someone said.

"June," several men pronounced in a ragged chorus.

I realized I was mimicking a class I'd attended with my grandfather years earlier in his assisted living center. It was a class for the senile and I had stupidly adopted the bit of curriculum I could remember.

"Roz asked me to teach and I don't know what to say," I admitted, casting a desperate glance at the door. "She should be here any minute."

"Tell us about yourself," Ezekiel suggested from the center of the semi-circle.

"*Me*? There's nothing very interesting about me."

Several of the men were clapping in rhythmic, sarcastic applause.

"Well, I live in New York now"—I felt sudden attention in the room—"but I grew up here in Jefferson City."

"You just visiting?" someone asked.

"Just slumming?"

"I'm here to visit someone. My husband died not too long ago. I had some vacation time and I decided to come back to my childhood home." While they thought that over, I jumped in with, "Now, tell me about *you*." I pointed to a young man directly in front of me.

Just then Roz limped in, swollen about the eyes. After a few words—the class clicked into place the minute she began speaking—she passed out copies of the poem. Students took turns reading aloud, then Roz led a discussion—"Is Frost talking about real fire? Real ice?"—before the class read aloud together.

I looked up from the poem. In the center of the semi-circle, the keystone of the arch, Ezekiel was reciting by heart.

At eleven-thirty when the other men left for lock-down, he remained in the classroom shelving books, this smart, erect old man still sturdy in the shoulders, arms, and legs. Sensing me behind him, he paused to adjust his wire-rimmed glasses, thumb and forefinger at the lens. "Do you remember your father?" Listening, he turned back and resumed his meticulous shelving.

I hesitated. I must not alienate him. He must not know how much I resented him or how clearly I understood that he would not relinquish his favored position with my mother.

"Yes. I remember him very well."

"And of course your mother."

The soothing hand that has never left the nape of my neck? A razor blade propped against my heart? A hot coal at the center of everything? Yes. Of course.

Ezekiel cocked his head to one side. "Do you know why she's here?"

"Yes."

"Do you understand what happened?"

"Somewhat." Had my mother put him up to this? To find out what her daughter knew?

He stood behind a student desk, holding onto the seat back with firm hands; with his mother-nearness hands. "She wants you to understand."

"For that, we need some time together," I said dryly.

He lifted his shoulders and arms, hands palm-up. "She doesn't want to leave the cell."

"Why not?"

"She can't explain it. I've asked her many times."

"You must have some idea."

He had no answer.

"Maybe you've made it too comfortable for her."

At this, he dropped his hands and turned away. I'd stung him.

"Or maybe she doesn't like change," I added.

"She feels guilty about everything," he said.

"Hasn't God forgiven her?"

"She doesn't think so."

"Tell her I want to understand." My vengeful feelings toward Ezekiel faltered. "Most of all," I whispered, "tell her I just want to be near her."

"It's not just you," he said. "She doesn't want to see anyone. She won't leave the cell, and she won't let anyone visit. 'You should talk to your daughter,' I tell her. 'Let her in.'"

I envied their intimacy. For there was no doubt that, while I lay alone, missing Walter, my mother was lying beside Ezekiel in the twin bed with the nice linens, or perhaps another bed, a double, a queen, a king, a continent-sized bed that Ezekiel had managed to appropriate and furnish with good-quality linens. My mother was actually a very lucky woman. I felt a stab of pity for my father who had not succeeded with her.

Sunlight cast a honey color on school desks and walls, while outside, through the windows, three inmates, their prison shirts stained with sweat, cut the grass with the very tool I'd been homesick for earlier: manual lawnmowers. The men were young and muscular, perhaps plucked from the population that had already been moved to the new prison. A guard lounging on the sidewalk looked bored.

"I'm going to step outside for a minute," Roz said from the desk at the front of the classroom. Ezekiel and I followed her out of the room, out of the building as she labored across the uneven ground. Whether this was originally rough terrain or relatively level acreage left chipped and ragged by the nineteenth-century prisoners who dug limestone from the site, I didn't know. A corrections officer followed lazily along the buckling sidewalk. After the air conditioning, this heat stunned the lungs and pores; at first the air was too hot for either breath or sweat.

Ahead, Roz reached a drop-off. The stone cottage trimmed with dark wood and precise brickwork was rooted in the gulley below. A cross of pebbles lay embedded in a concrete walk leading to its door. There was an attempt at landscaping: scraggily shrubs and rose bushes on either side of the cross.

In the shimmer of heat and light, I felt Tim's death and the deaths of condemneds I would never hear about. This small, dour building, this dark magnet, resisted the bright daylight all around us. I waited near Ezekiel.

"Since my mother doesn't want to leave her cell," I whispered, "I can come to *her*."

He turned to the right and gazed across the yard at the brooding stone hangar with its rows of cell windows. He snapped his fingers. "We can't do it just like that," he said. Then, "See all those windows?"

I didn't answer.

He pointed. "Sixth level. Eighth one over." The joints of his hands, his muscles, his fingertips contained strangeness and immediacy: he'd touched my mother.

"'A-Hall,'" he continued, his voice husky.

"How long have you been here, Ezekiel?"

"I really don't know. Too long to remember. I've more or less got the run of the place. Most people just have a house. I've had all this." Stretching out the same ropey arm, muscular in the forearm, loose above the elbow, he indicated the scope of his home.

"Do you have relatives?"

From the lower quarter of his eyes he seemed to test my ability to know him. "Yes. Some dead, some alive."

Roz finished her meditation, turned, and began setting one dogged foot in front of the other. Ezekiel and I fell in behind her and slowly retraced our steps up the uneven incline. Ezekiel looked across at the dormitory, the cell windows again, and lifted his hand. I waved, too, a gesture that left my heart pounding. The corrections officer had already reached the door. I felt his impatience to be inside the air conditioned building.

"Has my mother ever come up for parole?" I asked in an undertone.

"We both have." Back in the classroom, he added, "We've had chances. But you get set in your ways. And what would we

151

do? Where would we go?" He stared at me. "We'd have to be apart."

My eyes slid away from his.

"Don't worry about your mother," he said just before he left the room. "I take good care of her."

But I could take good care of her, too. Mabel Grant belonged with her daughter, as any parole officer would agree. I left the prison feeling competitive and feverishly acquisitive.

Fifteen

"Roz's ex-husband is very ill," I said. Steve had picked me up in his car to hear jazz in St. Louis. "As a matter of fact, she's in St. Louis right now."

He passed two noisy motorcycles traveling side by side. "She still sees her ex-husband?"

"Under normal circumstances, no. Not that she wouldn't like to. She's broken up over his illness."

Roz would be at the hospital now. A scene played itself: Simon Teal's surprised family making a space at the sick man's bedside for this single-breasted, red-headed, gimpy-legged, merry-eyed, sunshine-bearing woman. Puzzled glances: what is the ex-wife doing here? And in spite of—or because of—her strangeness, intensity, sympathy, they allow her to stay; are even glad for her support. Before she arrived they were despondent, but now the dying Simon Teal opens his eyes, breaks into a smile, and throws off the bedclothes. He tells Roz he has never stopped loving her. His present wife, happy to be relieved of a death bed scene, smiles benignly. The doctor comes in, examines the patient, frowns in disbelief, declares Simon cancer-free, and they all break into a chorus of "Oh, What a Beautiful Morning."

"All these highways," Steve pointed to the roadways, "funnel into one big road by the time you get to the Mississippi. You're daydreaming, Evelyn."

"I was thinking about Roz."

Between downtown skyscrapers, the giant steel arch on the Missouri side of the Mississippi River flashed in and out of view.

"I want you to see the cobblestone levee before we have dinner." Steve drove with pleasure. "Good music in that club," he said, pointing to an undistinguished building with an old brick façade.

The extra hour of light donated by the summer clock still

burned brightly. Soon the air would begin to blue and deepen and night would take back everything daylight saving time had worked to achieve.

We parked in front of a restaurant, dined on crab cakes and coleslaw, then walked a couple of blocks to a four-story brick building whose upper floors seemed abandoned. After lingering in front of the showroom crowded with paintings in a Harlem Renaissance style, we followed the side alley around to Jeremiah's Tavern.

Inside, a bar ran along the back of the cool, dark room. Jeremiah, a middle-aged African-American who, I guessed, had once been strong and well-hewn but whose years mixing drinks and breathing cigarette smoke contributed to loosened belly, shoulders, and jowls, stepped forward. The two men shook hands carelessly.

"Good to meet you," he said when Steve introduced me. Jeremiah possessed a tired smile and truthful face. "We've missed you, Steve. It's been too long." A few other patrons were scattered about the room eating peanuts from the shell and nursing drinks. The two men caught up on news before Steve and I seated ourselves at the bar.

"I used to be a regular customer," Steve said. "I've missed driving to St. Louis. Jeremiah and I have heard some good music together. We drove to East St. Louis a couple of times. He's always on the lookout for outstanding jazz."

"Why did you stop coming?"

He thought for a moment. "I used to bring a friend. When that ended, I got tired of coming by myself."

It was the first I'd heard him mention a relationship, the thing he said he wasn't good at. "You've never spoken much about your personal life," I murmured, "except for that situation with your cousin and uncle."

"I don't usually put my feelings into words." He smiled. "I'm an engineer."

"St. Louis is a great jazz town," he resumed after a silence. "Miles Davis is a Missourian, you know. Technically, he was born in Illinois, but we won't quibble. When he wanted to get serious about jazz, he crossed the bridge." A waitress took our drink orders. She was a small dark woman in tight white pants, as compact as her boss was slack. "Isn't that right, Tisha?"

"Whatever you say, Steve." I saw that, though he might not be good at relationships, he was not awkward with women.

"I've never spent much time in St. Louis," I said. "We'd go through Kansas City when we visited my mother's family. It's much different in Kansas."

"You don't have the Mississippi there," he said. "You don't have the French history. You're farther from the old slave trade." He took a swallow of his Scotch. "There's a bar in Kansas City with a white line painted down the middle of the room. The line divides Missouri from Kansas. During Prohibition when there was a raid by Missouri agents, the customers simply stepped over into Kansas, and vice-versa.

"No, really," he insisted when he saw my dubious expression. "It's the State Line Tavern on Southwest Boulevard." He twisted to survey the room behind us. He didn't care whether I believed him or not. He turned back. "My ex-wife sang with bands when we were young. I'd get a table up front. You went early because if you got there after eight you had to sit at the bar and you couldn't see the musicians. You'd be stuck there for the rest of the night.

"The smoke was thick. There was lots of smoking in those days. The drinks were good and the music went on all night. I had to go to work the next day but I didn't care. Back then I didn't need any sleep. I stayed for the music and to keep the guys away from my wife." He wagged his head slowly. "I couldn't keep the guys away, but I got a great education in jazz."

"How long were you married?"

"Just long enough for someone to get through my defenses."

"Did you ever hear Miles Davis play?" I prompted after a

while.

"Hell, yes... " He caught fire again. "I used to go with Jeremiah over to East St. Louis and listen to jazz till morning. He'd close up here and we'd head across the river. I tried to get something going in Jeff City, even invested in a club a friend opened, but we just didn't have the music scene."

"When was this?"

"A few years ago." He lifted his beer. "If you stick around we can make this a regular pilgrimage."

The musicians turned out to be just two: a pianist and a double-bass player. Steve frowned. "The percussion section seems to be indisposed." But I wasn't disappointed. I liked the subtle, quiet interplay of the two instruments. Their influence on each other was undisguised by a drumbeat. Staccato phrases circled and bounced off the wall, broke apart, then circled again, looking for a theme.

"What I like about jazz musicians is the way they listen to each other," Steve said. The bass player was briefly puzzled by a ragged piano line. His broad fingers hesitated above the finger board before finally landing with a thump.

"Could we have a booth?" Steve asked Jeremiah after the first set. Jeremiah motioned for Tisha to carry our drinks to a table against the wall. We slid in from either end of the banquette until we reached the middle. Sitting close to Steve, arm-to-arm, I felt peaceful and at rest. Even the music when it started up again was more settled, aware that if there wasn't a theme yet, one would come along by and by.

We stayed until nearly midnight. Walking to the car, we caught the scent of honeysuckle from a fugitive vine somewhere in all the brick and pavement. I thought I smelled the Mississippi River, dank, strong as brewed tea, flowing behind us.

All the way through St. Louis I wanted to duck under the seat belt and slide next to Steve; feel his arm against mine again. The engine sang. The weather was cool enough to have the air conditioner off and all four windows open. We passed the last of the suburbs and drove west through the night between fields of dark crops, breathing the sinus-clearing scent of irrigated earth on either side of the highway.

Steve misinterpreted my silence. "Daydreaming again?"

"Not at all," I said. Though not actually offended, I felt as if I'd been corrected. "Do I daydream a lot?"

"Well, yeah," he said. "I often catch you in a far-away place." In the silence that fell between us, his comment expanded to include more than my daydreams. After all, I was my mother's daughter. Perhaps there was a family gene for being not-here. No-where. A legacy of reminiscence. Reflection. Rumination. Daydreams. Hallucinations. Worse.

I leaned toward the passenger window. Mixed with spicy crops was the dark brown element of manure. A farmhouse in the distance, illuminated by a bright light high on a pole, seemed dangerously isolated in the middle of its acreage, vulnerable to rain, hail, and deviant travelers who could so easily leave the highway and drive slowly, quietly in second gear, up the dirt road that wasn't even graveled; that wouldn't give a warning crunch of approaching trouble. I pictured the prowler car pulsing along the capillary road that branched off this vein of state highway, itself connecting to the arterial interstate system where bad blood could circulate from the entire nation down to a little farmhouse with its mommy, daddy, and two darling babies asleep in their cribs...

I felt car sick. Steve reached across the seat. "Your hand is damp, Evelyn."

"Can you stop the car?"

He clicked on the hazards and pulled off the highway. As soon as we were outside, he began walking me up and down beside the road. An occasional car sped by. In the long moments between, we were dwarfed by the silence of open country and breezes that have several states to play in before they're stopped by mountains. On the shoulder we had to step over a low bank of dried mud bearing giant tire prints of a tractor. Weeds swayed in the ditch; frogs in the muddy water zipped and unzipped a thousand pockets of darkness.

"When I was a girl living with my grandparents, I used to pretend my mother had died," I said after we'd driven the last sixty miles and were coming in sight of Jefferson City. The lighted capitol dome glowed against the night sky. "I made up a story about how I would come back to town as a grown woman and learn that she hadn't died at all but was kidnapped and released when she and I were both old women."

"Helluva story," Steve said.

"And that we would live forever at 712 Capitol Avenue. And my father hadn't died in Mexico or even gone to Mexico. He'd been living in the house all along." Back then I hadn't known about Ezekiel. In a sense, she *had* been kidnapped. Kidnapped by Ezekiel. The story would end when she was freed by a force for good. That would be me.

The next afternoon Steve stopped his truck in front of my apartment and opened the passenger door for me. A manila envelope lay on the seat. It bore my name.

"What's that?" I asked, picking it up and climbing in.

"Something factual for you to look at." The word "factual" put me on alert. We sped through fields outlined in barbed-wire. The afternoon sun shone hard through the windshield. The smell of an oily rag on the floor of the hot cab tainted our ride to the farm.

When the truck had pulled up the steep hill in first gear and stopped in front of the house, we got out and climbed the steps. Steve laid the envelope on the near end of the porch bench and reached into his pocket for the house key. I gazed down the hill at the barn. Above the gambrel roof, a vulture lazily circled, scanning the property for something to feed on. I picked up the envelope and laid it on the railing where it would be available to anything flying by.

When Steve returned, he carried two plastic glasses of water and set them on the bench. He saw the envelope lying on the rail.

"Did you open it?"

I shook my head.

"I went to some trouble to get it." He sat down, picked up his glass, and held it in one hand. He leaned forward, resting his forearms on his thighs.

"I shouldn't have come," I said. "I'm sorry you drove all this way."

"The drive was easy compared to getting the papers."

"Where did you get them?"

"The Courthouse. The library." He picked up the envelope and turned it around and around in his hand. "When you talk to the Department of Corrections about parole you should know what you're talking about."

"But I already know."

"What do you know?"

I got up off the bench.

"It's good to face facts," Steve said again, as if I hadn't heard him the first time. I reached forward and picked up the envelope. I hadn't actually talked to anyone about parole yet, not the Department of Corrections, not a lawyer, certainly not Roz or Ezekiel, and most definitely not my mother. *It's hard to talk to someone you never see*, I almost said before rejecting it as self-pity. I laid the envelope on the bench and pressed the heels of my hands against my eyes. I did not need to know the details of May 22nd, 1962. "I appreciate the trouble you've gone to, but I'm not going to open it."

He took me by the shoulders. "I'll help you." Squatting in front of me, he laid the envelope on the floor boards of the porch and began to open it. I took it from him and held it on my lap while he spread the wings of the brass fastener and lifted the flap. I gave a half-hearted pull on the papers. He brought them all the way out.

In a black-and-white photograph, my mother looked dazed. Rail-thin, her hair pulled back in a tight bun, she stood on the Courthouse steps, squeezed between the bailiff and a lawyer, supported by both of them at the elbow. The bailiff looked large and uninterested. The lawyer was small and wore a hat, his lapels were wide, and a handkerchief in his jacket pocket was folded into a point. My mother wore a plain shirt and slacks.

"It's a prison uniform," I said. "Mother never wore slacks." I broke into a sweat. The papers slid to the porch. Steve put them back on my lap. He pulled out more paper, copies of news articles clipped together.

"Doctor's Wife Held in Insane Asylum While Awaiting Trial."
"Anderson Babies Drowned in Tub."
"Suspect Claims She Heard Voices."
"Daughter Escapes Murder Scene."

The newsprint moved away from me, then pulsed back in bold. I was reading and not reading, flying above the words, looking down from a great height at small letters.

"Daughter Evelyn, age 9, is reported to have followed her mother across the alley to the scene of the drowning. She then ran to a neighbor's house for help. The neighbor, Irene Winthrop, called the police…"

Steve had gotten up off his haunches to sit beside me on the bench.

"I don't remember this," I whispered. Yet I realized that all along I'd known my mother's hair had been loose; that before saying her prayers in the closet, she'd washed and set my hair in kid curlers; that when she came out of the closet and went downstairs, I'd quietly followed.

"She went in the Andersons' house without knocking," I said. "She knew you're not supposed to go in someone's house without knocking. I didn't knock on Mrs Winthrop's door, either. I was taking a chance, because Mrs Winthrop was mean and didn't like me. I just ran into her kitchen and she was there washing dishes—"

"What happened when you followed your mother?"

"I can't remember." But I did remember being terrified of Mrs Winthrop, of her thin, soapy hands and brown bathrobe. Her hair was yellowish-white—

"What happened across the alley?"

But I couldn't say. "Mrs Winthrop had a telephone niche between the kitchen and living room. I could see her piano through the little opening in the wall. She called the police to report me for coming inside her house without knocking."

Steve shook his head slowly, side to side.

"I did it because I was in a hurry."

"Why?" he said. "Why were you in a hurry?"

I didn't tell him why.

"Mrs Grant," I read silently, *"was heard to say that Jesus commanded her to do it."* I had an ungallant thought: my mother could have murdered me if she hadn't loved me more than the twins. A practical thought immediately followed: it is easier to murder babies than a nine-year-old.

I crumpled the pages in a spasmodic movement, then tried to straighten them again. In yet another photograph my father was emerging from the Courthouse, hovering behind my mother. Though he was overweight, he seemed insignificant; though his head was large, he came close to having no face at all.

A photograph showed Mrs Anderson weeping for her babies. *"The murder was apparently committed in a trance,"* the newspaper said, but the unnamed source did not elaborate.

"There's something wrong with me," I said to Steve. "I inherited something." I got up from the bench and stood swaying near the steps. He walked me to the sofa in the living room. We sat down side by side. "My father came once to see me in Idaho," I said. "There was a shiny green fly buzzing around the two of us in my grandparents' parlor. It flew in circles in front of my father's face and I couldn't see him. It was a loud fly.

We both knew someone was missing but we didn't talk about her."

Gripping the empty envelope, Steve held it up to my face. "What about her? What did she do at the Andersons'?" I'd never seen him impatient before. With one hand he clamped my arm above the elbow. Later there were bruises. To calm him, I took the envelope and stuffed the newspaper articles and papers back inside. He expected to hear something.

"She was praying when she picked up the babies and took them to the bathtub. She forgot I was there. And when she put the babies in the water and held them under"—my tongue smacked against the dry roof of my mouth—"she remembered I was there and pressed my forehead against the edge of the tub with her other hand. It hurt. My forehead hurt and the kid curlers hurt." The manila envelope slid onto the floor. "And when I ran away, she grabbed me by a curler, and it came out." I remembered the excruciating pain. "Some hair came out, too."

Unlike their usual neutrality, Steve's eyes were full of color and fire. His face was close to mine. I pulled my arm out of his grip and stared at the envelope on the floor. My mother killed two children and I'd watched her. It made her worse than I thought she was. It made *me* worse. An obituary would have been so much easier.

"I don't want her living with me!" I sobbed. "I've changed my mind."

"Don't worry about that now," he said. "Just see her again. Before the prison closes."

"Why should I?"

"Because that's why you're in Jefferson City."

I lifted my head. "Where will they send her?"

"Probably to Vandalia."

The world tipped toward Vandalia. Soon Capitol Avenue would no longer be the center of everything.

"Sharon called me last night," Roz said just before class started. Her face, usually pale from lack of sunlight, lack of exercise, lack of health, glowed. "She wants to come back to Jefferson City and finish high school." Her face brightened another watt. "I've told her she can stay at my house if she'd like."

I must have looked astonished.

"Why not?" she said, dimpling and sending off sparks of color into the monochromatic classroom.

"You and Sharon as mother and daughter?"

"Sure," she said briskly. "Why not?"

"You despised each other," I reminded her. "That day in the studio apartment when you were turning her beach robe inside-out and she yanked off her bikini top—"

"I know. I know." Roz ran her hand through her short, curly hair. "Evelyn," she said irritably, "people can make enormous changes."

"How?"

She handed a spelling list to a convict who came up with his hand out. His scarred face lapsed into trust before it hardened again. "Circumstances put Sharon and me together. We didn't have a choice." I followed her to the blackboard. "When we stood outside the prison that night, it didn't matter anymore what we thought of each other. We were just two people crying in each other's arms." She picked up a piece of chalk, laid it across her palm, and studied it. "We didn't have any opinions or plans. The wall was the only thing holding us up. The wall and each other. That was all there was to it."

She turned to write on the board: "Spelling test. Second chance." I took a seat beside one of the students who began explaining to me what he'd just read. I was impressed by his comprehension. I couldn't have done half as well summarizing what Roz had just said to me. I couldn't imagine being dramatically changed like Roz and Sharon at the wall.

After class I walked as far as the Governor's Mansion and beyond. I hated returning home to rooms that were supposed to have filled my emptiness. Why had I thought emptiness could fill emptiness?

I lingered at the corner of Monroe and Capitol, then climbed the steps of the Methodist Church. I entered the sanctuary, sat down in a pew, and planted my feet slightly apart. Seeking forgetfulness, complete erasure of the Anderson bathtub, I bowed my head and charged into meditation.

But my prayers were balky and gave no satisfaction. After a few minutes I stood and, compelled to move about, took the back stairs to the church basement where I stalked through a series of Sunday School rooms. Fragments of memorized literature flitted through my mind: the Lord's Prayer, the Twenty-Third Psalm, John 3:16. I could almost hear "Jesus loves me, this I know" being sung by the sweet voices of children. I smelled graham crackers and Kool-Aid.

Eventually the waving flag of my mind stopped snapping and hung limp. I was the definition of emptiness. But soon the wind picked up again and the flag was once more whipping on its pole. I began to blame Walter. I'd adopted his lack of faith. But whereas his unbelief had been buttressed by self-confidence, philosophy, vast reading, I had no such props. Without him, I was alone. How cruel of him to die first. Not only had I been left husband-less and mother-less, but God-less, too.

Don't despair, I heard him say as I cut through the kitchen with its commercial-size appliances and meaty scents of past meals. *Don't despair, Evelyn.* His language sounded biblical, something he was not. *If you need God, darling, then God is here.*

No, I said. *I need you, Walter.*

Remember our ski trip? he said. *1985? The trip to Colorado?*

Nothing was further from my thoughts.

You didn't think you could manage the slope.

Mostly I remember our night in bed, I admitted. *I didn't like skiing. But I liked you.*

In real life he would have laughed. *That's my point,* he said. *It was a difficult slope. The sex was part of the slope.*

Walter always said "sex" instead of "lovemaking," the word I preferred. Now I used his word. *I have always preferred sex to skiing, Walter. And sex to no-sex. Life to death. You to not-you.*

Stumbling out of church, I began walking uphill toward town. As I approached High Street I noticed tiny barred windows nearly hidden at the back of the Courthouse. They overlooked a dismal alley separating the county jail from First Methodist. While waiting for her trial to end, my mother must have been kept there, a practice run for a life sentence just a few blocks away. A last chance to catch a glimpse of stained glass windows. On the corner, I stopped at the public face of the Courthouse, dignified by its rococo clock tower, peaked roof, cement tracery. Though beautiful, the building was unforgiving. It was here, not in the church, that my mother had been judged.

I turned toward the entrance and courtroom inside. A sign in the marble lobby directed me to the second floor. In one of the two courtrooms a trial was taking place. The other was still and unused. Faint light came through its high windows, though most of the daylight was held back by velvet drapes swagged and caught back at the sills by cords.

I rested my hand on a newel post and lowered myself onto the hard wood. Straight ahead was the judge's bench, backed by the state and national flags. To the right, the jury box. Directly in front, counsel tables. Mabel Grant must have sat at one of these. I felt her presence. Time didn't pass; it no longer existed. I was resting my head against her unreliable heartbeat. The woman's insanity laid me low. I blotted my damp hairline with a handkerchief and bowed my head. If my mind had been an orchestra and the dead babies a theme played by, say, the oboe, nasal, insistent, disturbingly edgy, then every time its melody insinuated itself into my head—see the infants being held under the bathwater, look at their little faces, watch your mother's hair loosened from the hair pins—sounds of the full orchestra tumbled in: violins keening, trombones braying, drums rattling.

The oboe must be silenced.

Over the sick pounding of my heart, the orchestra tuned. Eventually the cacophony faded and I sat quietly. I heard the public accusation:

"State of Missouri, Plaintiff, against Mabel Grant, Defendant."

I imagined the days-long trial, heard the verdict, and accepted it.

I stood abruptly. Walking down Capitol Avenue in the fading sunlight, I paused in front of my house and crossed the street. When I reached the prison wall, I leaned against its still-warm limestone, rough and porous. After remaining there for a time, as close to my mother as I could get, I re-crossed the street and returned home for my parents since they had not been able to do it for themselves.

Sixteen

I slept fitfully and woke the next morning. I could not bear more introspection, more Jefferson City, more prison, more forgiveness or non-forgiveness, more—or less—mother: I want her, I don't want her. Almost as upsetting as my mother's and my abandonment of each other was our lack of something Roz and Sharon possessed: resilience. At ten I called a taxi.

"Where to?" said the driver. It was the same driver who had met my train.

"The bus station."

"Had enough of us, have you?"

I smiled wanly. I'd had enough of myself.

The woman behind the Greyhound counter looked puzzled when I said, "One ticket for the next eastbound bus." Amused, even.

"Southeast? Northeast? Where you headed?" Years of smoking had given her a woolen voice and particle-rich cough.

"New York City."

"Round-trip?"

"One-way." I'd achieved what my children called closure. Closure doesn't necessarily mean success. It doesn't necessarily mean reconciliation. It can mean failure.

My rent was paid, and I owed nothing to anyone. I would learn to live with myself. *Just as I am.*

I had to wait two and a half hours. The vending machine produced a stale cheese sandwich. I chewed and stared out the dingy windows at hickory trees lining the edge of the parking lot, their leaves almost gray, as if maintaining plump greenness through the summer had become a chore. I envied them the certainty of the seasons. Every fall they would lose their leaves; every spring, regain them. They didn't have to wonder what they were made of; what their upbringing and genes would incline them to do. They didn't have to ask themselves if living in an empty apartment above lawyers' offices was strange, not unlike turning a sewing room into a chapel.

When the bus rolled into its diagonal parking slot against the building, I nearly cried from relief. I left my bags beside the luggage compartment and climbed on. Except for food and bathroom stops, I didn't climb off again until the next day. I never found a town I liked, possibly because, from Jefferson City to somewhere in Ohio, I did nothing but sleep. I would wake to find a seatmate beside me, sleep again, and wake with a different mate or none at all. The sun would be at the lip of the flaming horizon, and the next time I woke, I was traveling through dark farmland that extended, it seemed, to the end of the world. Now and then I stumbled off the bus for bottled water, a sandwich, a bathroom. My teeth needed brushing. The window beside me was smudged from someone's unwashed head lolling against the glass: my own. Somewhere in Ohio I called my son, then my daughter.

"We've been wondering why we couldn't reach you," they each said in their own way. "We were beginning to worry." I assured them I was fine and that I'd taken a short trip to see more of Missouri.

"Where are you now?" Since I wasn't sure what state I was in, I said, "Springfield, and I'm just now heading back to Jefferson City." It wasn't a total lie. Every state has a Springfield.

Somewhere in Indiana I disembarked and took a motel room. I had a bath and meal; hand-washed the clothes I'd been wearing; slept in a real bed. Though saturated with sleep, some inner part of me had remained awake. Never mind my children's closure, the church's supposed redemption, Roz's lust for life, Sharon's adaptability, Steve's facts. This was my mother's and my business. No, *my* business since my mother didn't care. I really hadn't finished with Jefferson City. As soon as I got back to town I would make an appointment with the Department of Corrections. Next, I would go shopping. My mother and I needed more than an air mattress, card table, and folding chairs. The two of us weren't finished with each other yet. Correction: I wasn't finished with her. It was clear she was finished with me.

I called Roz.

"Where are you, Evelyn?"

"In Indiana."

"Indiana! You need to come home right away. They're moving your mother to the women's prison in Vandalia. Ezekiel and I can't do a thing about it."

As my bus rolled into Jefferson City, late afternoon was sliding into a round, warm evening. Nighttime came earlier and earlier in these last days of August. Stores were selling back-to-school supplies. The memory of shopping with my mother for new pink erasers, No. 2 pencils, the annual paint box, all struck with such freshness that I could hardly wait to re-create our home and fill it with furniture, china, linens, and whatever art I could scare up along High Street. Fresh flowers, of course.

I spent a sleepless night. I'd slept better on the bus. Cooking cereal the next morning, stirring raisins into the panting, bubbling oats, I realized how easy it would be to brood my way through the last twenty-five percent of my life. My parents had already failed more than fifty percent of theirs. Our family's grade point average was nothing to write home about. The numbers had to change.

After breakfast, still in my nightgown, I walked through the rooms, surveying the monochromatic walls, considering how to make the empty spaces attractive not only for myself and my mother, but for the Corrections people, too. They might inspect the apartment.

What kind of art would the Department like? I called the Administration Office. A recording informed me they wouldn't open until 9:00 a.m. Grateful for the one-hour reprieve, I selected navy-blue slacks and a plain white blouse in which to appear before the Warden.

I want to bring my mother home with me, I imagined myself saying, preempting any sign of skepticism in his jaded eye. *She's too old to be moved to the Vandalia prison. I live just across the street, you know. In our original home.*

The Warden would smile, immediately grasping the salient points I left unsaid. *Your mother never wanted to leave prison before,* he'd reply. *She's never wanted to leave Ezekiel. But this time I know she'll want to leave. After all, she'll be living with you. And by the way*—he closed one official eye—*remember: the family that prays together stays together.*

I looked at my watch. There was time to try church again; try it as often as necessary until it took. Inoculation against unbelief. A pathway for change. God would wash away doubt and I would love Him and believe in Jesus. I would understand my mother and forgive her. The prison administrator would consider me a fit parent for my parent. I would be a child, lost, then found, like the little lamb in the stained-glass window, changed into a high-functioning adult. The church and I would accept each other. And since the church had failed my mother who worshipped faithfully for years and yet ended up committing a terrible sin for which she'd spent forty-two years in the penitentiary, here was God's chance to redeem Himself.

I was already praying when I stepped off Capitol Avenue and into First Methodist. I opened the double doors of the sanctuary and slipped once again into my mother's pew. I was breathing hard. *Our Father who art in Heaven* gave way to *talk to my mother, God. Please talk to her.* After a few more minutes the incantation changed to *God, God, God, I want my mother.* Abruptly I stopped forming words and simply sat.

I must have stayed all afternoon. The organist began making clacking, wooden sounds in the organ loft, opening up the console before choir practice, setting music on the rack, rustling pages. There was a musical squawk as he accidentally hit the keyboard. Arpeggios made the empty church shake, hum, and buzz with vibrations as his feet flew up and down the bass pedals. A Bach fugue opened out into the sanctuary but broke off impulsively, as if he really didn't need to practice. He began a quiet hymn,

"*I come to the garden alone…* "

It was a hymn my mother had loved. I, myself, had always thought it sentimental.

"*… while the dew is still on the roses. And the voice I hear falling on my ear …* "

It drained off into an enviable but shallow certitude that sounded like jogging:

"*And He walks with me and He talks with me…*"

No one was walking and talking and jogging with me. And certainly no one was calling me His own. Perhaps if I'd been surrounded by a congregation, if others' prayers had brushed against mine, oiling my spiritual mechanism, mixing my own feeble worship with the larger, stronger mix, I might have gained something. But as it was, I experienced only irritation. An entire afternoon spent in a pew praying and I had only irritation to show for it.

I stood up, stiff, and with a full bladder. I saw no one on my way to the women's room. I passed stairways, corridors, and doorways, components of a lifeless building. In spite of my great need, First Methodist hadn't helped me. In the bathroom I cried and voided, voided and cried, and cursed my mother and my mother's church for abandoning her, and now me.

In the anteroom of the restroom I sat down in a shabby wicker rocking chair someone had probably donated to the church. It might have been used in the nursery until something newer and better came along. After several minutes of silence that more resembled prayer than my entire afternoon in the sanctuary, I stood and remained in the anteroom until the empty chair stopped rocking. I let myself out of the church by a side door and walked home, wrung out, actually thirsty from having cried so much. I climbed the outside staircase of my old house, into the living room, on into the guest room, and straight to the walk-in closet.

The day was almost gone and I was still paralyzed.

The window through which airy, whipped sunlight had once foamed and spilled onto my mother's high forehead was dingy now. A nearly full moon lifted itself above Jefferson City. Centered in the dusty closet window, it was of a reddish hue. Across the street my mother would be seeing the same moon. I avoided the rugs and sat directly on the hardwood floor. Stretching out my legs, bracing my arms and hands behind me, I locked myself in place by my own elbows. Nothing passed through my mind. No satisfaction. No consolation. No desolation, either. No closure, reconciliation, or decisive thought. I experienced emptiness. Nothing more.

And I still hadn't called the prison administrator.

The next morning I was back in the literacy class, moving with Roz among the students. Much of the hour was spent at three computers lined up on a long table: an old desktop model that belonged to the prison, and two equally old laptops that belonged to Roz. The men took turns at the keyboards, pecking out sentences. Roz, she of the old computers, of begged and borrowed supplies, shunted her bulk and enthusiasm from student to student, correcting here, encouraging there.

Ezekiel entered the classroom.

"Your mother wants to see you, Mrs Williams," he said in a broken voice. I turned my head so swiftly that something snapped in my neck. Around us, inmates worked. The classroom hummed and buzzed with the effort to read and write.

Roz had overheard. "Oh, God," she said, coming up beside us. "What's happened?"

"They're moving her to Vandalia," Ezekiel said, "and they're moving me to the new prison. Tomorrow." As if to provide the strength, the starch he needed to face change, Roz stepped close to him. Moisture had broken out on her forehead and her breathing was noticeable. He waved her away and gestured toward the buildings and grounds surrounding us. "They're emptying us out. I can't do a thing about it." His eyes flashed, shot to one side, and back again. The control over his life that he'd gradually accumulated through the years, that he'd built up like a handsome, serviceable glaze over his original skin, was cracking. No more roaming freely through the penitentiary, a trusty on close terms with the guards. I saw the bad news in his body. He'd lost control over where he and my mother would be housed, and separation from her was like physical pain. He seemed old today; coming loose from his skeleton. He favored his right side. He'd lost height. I thought he might have had a small stroke.

We locked eyes. "Talk to the Warden, even the Governor," he pleaded. "Tell them how old she is and how she's worked in the hospital ward. She deserves to stay in Jefferson City." Roz remained quiet, not because she was restraining herself, but because Ezekiel wouldn't let her intervene. "I can take care of her in the new prison," he said. "I've been a trusty all these years

"I called the Warden," I said, omitting the fact that I'd gotten a recording and hadn't called back. "I wanted her to be paroled and come across the street to live with me."

"Yes, yes," Ezekiel said with low-level excitement that had potential for growth. "She'd be in her old home. She could visit me."

"At one point I was hoping you could both be paroled and come across the street to live with me," I said ill-advisedly. An imagined future with my mother flashed so brightly across his face that I saw his private movie. He waited for me to say more: *I'll talk to the administration this afternoon, I'll tell them all about you and my mother and your history here. You and my mother will be on the other side of the wall in no time.* When I didn't, the brown went out of his eyes; the black out of his skin. He looked gray. Diluted.

"Does she want to see me," I said, "or do *you* want me to see her?"

His eyes blazed just before he looked away.

Surely guilt explained why she still didn't want to see me. Or was it some disability deeper than guilt? Something that propelled her to run from her husband and child? To hide in hallucination? "Tell my mother not to blame herself," I blurted, and grabbed for Ezekiel's hand. "Tell her Abraham heard a voice, too." I remembered a visual aid from Sunday School, the flannel picture board, with Abraham's knife upraised against his own child. *Take now thy son, thine only son Isaac, whom thou lovest.* At the last minute God's heavenly fist had descended from the sky and punched through the fluffy flannel-cloth clouds to stop the murder.

But He had not drained the bathwater in time to save the babies. He had not saved my mother's mind.

"You got to be careful about God's voice," Ezekiel said. "I tell her: 'Don't believe everything you hear, Mabel.'" He took off his glasses and massaged his eyes. "You have to talk to her, Mrs Williams! Bring her back to her senses!"

"She hasn't been in her senses for a long time, Ezekiel," I said quietly.

"Visit her in Vandalia!" he cried. "Tell her about me! Then come back and tell me about *her*!"

"She doesn't realize how much she'll miss you, Ezekiel," I said.

"She'll find someone else," he said bitterly.

"It's a women's prison," I said.

"She'll find someone else. There's always competition for her. I had to fight 'em off." He looked proud for a moment. "God made her the way she is. He made her desirable but He didn't give her fire of her own." His love, protection, the decorated cell, the high-jacked bed linens had not won him my mother's heart.

Her heart was stone.

Reaching out and cupping Roz's elbow, he seemed to be rummaging for a thought that might elude him if he didn't express it right away. "Roz understands what's inside and outside the wall. She passes through it over and over again. She climbs over and digs under it every day." He released her, placed his hands together palm to palm, and brought the tips of his fingers to his chin. "You know, limestone is made of ground-up fossils. The wall is fossils. Everything is ground up over millions of years. Everything is ground up again and again."

I waited for him to make his point. But apparently he'd reached the limit of what he knew about limestone because he touched Roz lightly one more time, turned, and walked out of the classroom.

Seventeen

"How long has Ezekiel been looking after her?" I asked.

Roz leaned back in the upholstered arm chair I'd purchased during those frenzied days in summer when I'd daydreamed about bringing my mother across the street to live with me. "Long before I started teaching at the prison."

From one end of a sofa capacious enough to accommodate an elderly mother, grown children, prospective grandchildren—prospective great-grandchildren, if you looked at it from my mother's point of view—as well as innumerable guests I'd thought she and I would entertain in the years ahead, I watched Roz help herself to coffee cake I'd baked in a bundt pan and served on new dessert plates decorated with the State bird. Mentally I counted the towel sets stacked in the linen closet: bath towels, hand towels, wash cloths. Bed sheets with their presewn corners stretched tautly over mattresses in the fully furnished bedrooms. Knives, forks, spoons, salad forks, ice tea spoons lay flat in divided drawers. Heavy cookware, including a turkey roaster for holidays, sat on bottom shelves of the kitchen cabinets.

"All those years I was married and raising children, my mother was with Ezekiel."

"Your mother has not been alone."

"And while I was living alone here across the street, she was being protected by a man who not only loves her, but decorates her prison cell."

"I tried to get you and your mother together as soon as I realized who you were. I knew Ezekiel could help you."

"Are you talking about your manipulations to woo me into the classroom?"

"I wanted you inside the walls where you could meet Ezekiel, and then your mother."

"You knew she would never show up for visiting hours."

Roz shrugged. "Everyone knows she's a hermit."

"I guess I should thank you," I said. "I don't know why you went to so much trouble."

She smiled cryptically. "It wasn't just for you. It was for me, too. I don't have a life of my own. I require other people. I require plans and projects."

"You seem very alive to me," I said. "Maybe you don't need to work so hard at having a life."

"Oh, but I do. People aren't attracted to me until they need me. I was born to help, and so that's what I do."

"Even if it's not wanted?"

She looked at me as if I were a problem easily fixed. "We don't always know when we need help, Evelyn."

"I'll admit I was defensive," I said. "Am defensive. But I didn't want someone else to find my mother for me. I resented your help. I'm sorry now."

She ignored my apology. "My husband left me," she said. "My baby died. Tim was executed. Cancer is always circling. Would you still say I don't need to work to have a life?"

"I see what you mean."

"And what now?" she said in her let's-have-a-project tone. "I may not need a teaching assistant, strictly speaking, but class goes much better when you're there, Evelyn. You can't give students too much attention when they're learning to read. The class is about to start in the new prison. Ezekiel's there. He'll help us. You and I might even start a class in Vandalia. Drive there two or three times a week. It's not far."

The thought of riding on the highway with Roz was more alarming than taking on a new prison. Still, a tiny firecracker of hope went off in my mind. From Vandalia I could carry back news of my mother to Ezekiel, and vice-versa. Because, of course, my mother would welcome my visits in Vandalia. Without Ezekiel, she'd be lonely. We'd start off on a new footing.

Roz studied my art-filled walls slowly and thoroughly. "What are you going to do with yourself here in Jefferson City?" she said after a while.

"I don't know. I can't mourn forever. Not with you around the corner. You won't let me sit and stew."

"I believe in action."

"Well... " I didn't believe in action any more than I believed in inaction.

"Do something, even if it's wrong. That's my motto."

I wasn't prepared to go that far. My mother had done something wrong and it hadn't turned out well for any of us.

"I miss the old prison," Roz said, ruminating between bites of cake. "I liked crossing the street and being right there at the front gate. Even though prison is nothing to be proud of, I liked the old buildings. They had dignity. A deplorable dignity, I know, but still dignity. Like Ezekiel and your mother. Old, with dignity."

"Deplorable dignity," I said.

"Not everyone would agree with me about the dignity," Roz said. "Being behind the walls changes the way you think about prisoners."

"What makes you think my mother has dignity?"

"Well, she has a mind of her own. She's beyond punishment."

"She lost her mind," I said.

Roz looked out the window. I followed her eyes. I'd recently put up drapes. At night they shut out what I still thought of as working floodlights of a working prison.

"We don't have to forget her just because she's been transferred to Vandalia, you know."

I nodded dubiously.

Wrapping her hands first around one knee, then the other, she lifted each leg until both were supported by my brand-new tufted hassock. She adjusted her scarves, brushed crumbs from her lap, and looked at me with an eye bright as a bead. "After we've volunteered to teach in Vandalia for a while, they might eventually pay us. We can expand our work," she said.

"God, Roz."

"Have I interfered all along?" She tied, then untied, the scarf at her throat. "I thought I was helping." I'd offended her.

"Maybe you were helping. Maybe you weren't. It was a project. But I wish I'd never tried to see my mother again." I stopped and looked around the room. "Of course, if I hadn't, I wouldn't have fixed up this apartment."

Roz scanned the walls quickly. "Very nice," she murmured with automatic good manners.

"I wouldn't have left New York, either." It was as close as I'd come to admitting Jefferson City had changed me. But, "Oh, Roz," I said, "let's not try again."

"Vandalia is within easy driving distance, Evelyn."

I shook my head and picked up the used plates. "Steve will be here soon." We'd set this time for a post-mortem on our Moreau Heights grade school event held the preceding weekend. Bouncing back from the execution, Steve had asked Roz and me to help him re-plan the hundred-year celebration.

"We've gotten a bunch of mail," he said after climbing the outside staircase and letting himself in. "Lots of thank-you's." While he shed his jacket and seated himself, I brought out the committee checkbook and bills along with more coffee cake. "It was a nice occasion," he said. "Cider-sweet weekend." He smiled modestly at his foray into poetry. A bite of cake trembled on the end of his fork. "I'm developing a tremor," he noted, dispassionately studying the wavering fork. "Thank God it doesn't affect the large muscles."

"We've all got some minor condition or other," Roz said. I wouldn't have described her bout with cancer as a minor condition, but I admired her understatement. A twinge of bursitis distracted me.

"I've heard about your farm, Steve," Roz said, refusing to

discuss health. "You've got some hunting friends in Corrections who talk about it."

"Oh, yeah. Several of us hunt on my property every year." He chewed meditatively, finished the cake, and laid down his fork. "How long have we been neighbors here on Capitol Avenue?" he asked her.

"Over twenty years. I watched your apartment house go up. Remember?"

"And what do you think of it? Pro or con?"

"Personally, I like old buildings. I liked your old family home. But I don't object to the building, per se. I know Sharon Riley liked her studio apartment."

"What's she doing now since…?"

A vase holding bright chrysanthemums caught the autumn sun coming through my windows. Roz's face was like a second bouquet. "Living with me," she said. "She's taken the place of Tim Anguin in my life. You might get to see her soon. I left a note saying I was here. She likes to know where I am. Sticks to me like flypaper."

With his hand still shaking slightly, Steve adjusted his glasses and turned his attention to the bills resting on the sofa between us. The engineer was ready to think about numbers.

But Roz wasn't. "Almost all those people who came to the centennial"—she gestured toward the paperwork, then outward toward the school and its former students—"have children and grandchildren. They're busy and productive… " I sensed she was entering a spiral of self-criticism, as if her moment of joy and self-respect had begun to erode the moment it rose to the surface.

"Hold on," said Steve. "You're busy and productive."

"True. But I really need these special events to keep me going. Teaching and meetings and public occasions… "

With a hint of exasperation Steve said, "And what about my former tenant? She obviously thinks the world of you. You have an excellent life, Roz." He turned to me. "Wouldn't you say she has an excellent life?"

"Excellent life," I said.

"I'd say we all have an excellent life," he added. For me, his words intensified the light and the chrysanthemums. There was a knock on the door and Sharon entered. Frothy attention from the three of us splashed about her as she dropped her back pack full of books onto a chair in the corner.

Wonderful to see you, so glad you're back in Jefferson City, how marvelous to be young and in high school, to have put Tim's death behind you, to have overcome grief, your whole life ahead of you, etc., etc., we might as well have been saying aloud. Our faces gleamed. If she wasn't aware that we were pinning our hopes on her, on youth, health, the future, she was at least aware of being the center of interest.

"Want a piece of cake?" I said, reducing my admiration to the size of a dessert plate. I was already half-way to the kitchen.

"I just came to check on Roz." There was no irony. I stuck to my offer and returned with cake and coffee that Sharon ultimately left untouched on the side table. I could see Roz struggle against a maternal impulse: *Say thank you,* or worse, *Eat the cake the nice lady fixed for you.*

"I hear you're going to school in Jeff City now," Steve said. "If you ever need a reference, I can recommend you as a good tenant."

I can recommend you as a resilient young woman, I wanted to say. We all wanted to recommend her for something, but for what, we would have to wait until she, herself, knew.

"What time will you be home?" Roz asked.

"Six-thirty. A couple of people are helping me catch up in trig."

"Trigonometry!" I said with respect.

"I'm behind where I should be," she said. "English is even worse." Though her jaw was still wide, her arms lean, Sharon had become a more limber girl, with less mandible and sinew.

Her green eyes were softer, her skin and hair healthier. "Except Hemingway," she added. "I like Hemingway."

"I liked Hemingway," Steve said. "*The Old Man and the Sea.*"

"Steve fishes," Roz said. "And he has a farm where he hunts."

"Deer?" said Sharon. "My dad hunts."

"By the way, does he want his small-size refrigerator back?" Steve asked. "He brought it for you. It's still in the apartment."

She stood and picked up her book bag. The straps dangled above the hardwood floor. "That's where the refrigerator came from?"

"You bet. It's still there."

Was the shadow that crossed her face some bit of Tim Anguin left behind? Was she remembering that he'd still been alive when the refrigerator appeared in her apartment? Or was it her parents that made her sad?

She turned toward Roz. "Do you want a small refrigerator?"

"We could put it in your room. For snacks. Or maybe your parents could drive up for a visit and take it back with them."

Sharon was giving the matter a surprising amount of thought. I could see Steve trying to evaluate the situation.

"I guess you didn't expect your parents to drive so far with a refrigerator," I said.

"Was it a week day?" she asked Steve. "Maybe I was at work."

"It was a week day, I think." He squinted a little and looked at her from his place on the sofa. "What's the significance of the refrigerator?"

"My dad brought it on a week day. He knew I wouldn't be home. He didn't want to see me."

"It's a long way to drive," Steve said, "to make sure you don't see somebody."

"Did he say anything? Did he leave a message?"

"No. It was an anonymous gift."

She took several steps closer to Steve. "My dad didn't want me living away from home."

"Did he pay your rent?" Steve asked. "It was always on time."

With saucy pride Sharon tilted her head. "I had a job. I paid it myself."

"Did your folks know about Tim?"

Sharon looked toward the window, though she couldn't see her old apartment from where she was sitting. "My dad knew because Tim wrote him a postcard and said he was innocent and when he got out of prison he was going to marry me."

"Were you planning on marrying him if he got out?" Steve asked.

"Oh, yes."

Roz and I looked from Steve to Sharon and back again.

"Well, your dad probably didn't know what to say," Steve said, "or if he did, he didn't know how to say it."

"He never minded saying stuff before."

"This was more serious," said Steve, ever the man for facts. "Tim murdered two women."

Sharon looked abashed, then defiant. "You'd have to see my dad to understand," she said.

"I've seen him," Steve said.

Roz shifted her legs on the hassock, lay back against the chair cushion, and closed her eyes.

"Well, 'bye," Sharon said. Roz stirred, opened her eyes, and waved. The screen door creaked as the girl let herself out. On the landing she wriggled into the back pack and gave a small leap in place to distribute the weight. Her steps grew faint down the outside stairway, and then she was gone. Steve began looking through the stack of bills and receipts. We were quiet and let Roz rest in the warmth of the syrupy light flowing through the room.

Epilogue

In the 1830s, with picks and shovels, inmates excavated stone and formed it into brick. Over the years, brick by brick, row by row, they walled themselves inside their self-shaped home. Stone buildings, corridors, cells rose from the ground. Kitchens, mess halls, laundries, infirmary were carved from sediment.

Almost two centuries later, the prison is empty; the limestone is crumbling. Buried with the rubble, with the remains of inmates who preceded them, my mother and Ezekiel rest among green shoots. The Missouri River floods now and again, and fish swim between graves. From my front room I look out at the rusting guard towers and think back to when the limestone wall disappeared behind our closed drapes every evening and reappeared each morning, before my mother was taken away.

ABOUT THE AUTHOR

Marlene Lee has worked as a court reporter, teacher, college instructor, and writer. A graduate of Kansas Wesleyan University (BA), University of Kansas (MA), and Brooklyn College (MFA), she currently lives in Columbia, Missouri and New York City. After graduating from Kansas Wesleyan, she taught English at Salina Senior High School. Her poems, stories, and essays have appeared in numerous publications.

Other books by Marlene Lee:

The Absent Woman

Published by Holland House April 2013

Virginia Johnstone doesn't need a rest, she needs a change; not comfort, but purpose. Divorced, and a visitor in her children's lives, she decides to leave Seattle and spend three months in the harbor town of Hilliard. There, on the edge of Puget Sound, she sublets rooms in an old hotel, rooms belonging to a woman who has vanished without explanation. In search of someone who can take her piano-playing to the next level, Virginia encounters Twilah Chan, an inspiring teacher and disturbing presence. Twilah's son, Greg, an exciting but also disturbing presence, re-awakens Virginia's romantic life. When she discovers a connection between the absent woman of the old hotel, Twilah, and Greg, she must decide whether to pursue the uncertain course she has set for herself or return to the safety of Seattle.

In a novel which is both elegiac and passionate, insightful and wryly humorous, Marlene Lee explores the need for change and the emotional consequences of leaving an old life in order to embrace a new one.

Praise for The Absent Woman:

"I couldn't put down The Absent Woman. I relished every scene, every word. It's one of the most compelling novels that I've read..."
    Ella Leffland, author of *Rumors of Peace; The Knight, Death, and the Devi*l, and others

"Lee writes quite beautifully, with grace and wit and precision. I thought it was a very brave book, and very honest. Virginia's feelings about leaving her boys were especially resonant. And she writes about music wonderfully. The book will stay with me for a long time."
    Alex George, author of A Good American

In Marlene Lee's psychologically astute debut, THE ABSENT WOMAN, Virginia Johnstone finds herself straining against the limitations of her existence as a comfortable suburban wife and mother. She leaves her husband and her boys to embark on a sometimes exhilarating, sometimes excruciating, and always compelling journey of self-examination. In lucid prose, Lee tells a marvelous story with echoes of Kate Chopin's THE AWAKENING."
    Keija Parsinnen, author of *The Ruins of Us*.

Rebecca's Road

Published by Holland House November 2013

"You're beginning to understand the world."
"Am I? Then I don't like it."
"That's precisely why your mother and I kept it from you."

Rebecca has always been looked after, cared for, shielded from the world; to avoid the realities, Mother would take her shopping, and her parents built a wing of their house just for her. But now Mother is dead and Rebecca, fifty years old, wants to take one of those trips she and Mother had often talked about. So she bargains with her father for the trust money he is withholding and buys a motor home in which she sets off to learn about life, love, and the world beyond the family peach orchard; to see if there is a different Rebecca to be found along the way.

Illustrated by B Lloyd